MURDER IN PARADISE

MURDER IN PARADISE

An Inspector Faro Mystery

Alanna Knight

CHIVERS

British Library Cataloguing in Publication Data available

This Large Print edition published by BBC Audiobooks Ltd, Bath, 2009.
Published by arrangement with Allison & Busby Ltd.

U.K. Hardcover ISBN 978 1 408 43292 1
U.K. Softcover ISBN 978 1 408 43293 8

Printed and bound in Great Britain by
CPI Antony Rowe, Chippenham and Eastbourne

For Fran Nicholson,
with love

PROLOGUE

Rich and famous, poor and obscure, whatever the condition there is no escape. Every memory holds forbidden places, places of shame or terror not willingly revisited, sometimes merely a cruel word said in haste and never forgotten, a mean or thoughtless action, but sometimes that memory is a monster, foul murder left untried.

Fate had not forgotten Jeremy Faro and the dark shadow might have remained where it had lain, buried deep for thirty years of a brilliant career in the Edinburgh Police Force. Ironically, it was his true love, his dearest companion Imogen Crowe, who threw open the door and let his demon escape and turned the knife in the wound once more.

After his retirement as chief inspector in the 1880s, Faro travelled far and wide with the always restless Imogen, and was made welcome in so many artistic groups and political societies. Inevitably their brief return visits to Scotland were via London where Imogen had access to a friend's apartment in Park Lane.

Imogen loved London, she loved the concerts, the galleries and the high living. Faro didn't and told her that the gallery openings, the lavish society occasions, with Imogen and himself as honoured guests, were overcrowded and overheated, and, most important, his feet (from years of chasing criminals) soon hurt and the conversations shouted across crowded rooms bored him. He was a little reluctant to admit to his forty-year-old companion that he did not always hear what was being said in the din and that an Orcadian's lifetime dedication to drams of whisky regarded champagne with a cautious dislike.

Imogen listened, sighed and kissed him fondly. She loved people, was always the writer, searching, gathering material for another travel book—another biography—that was her lifeblood. She couldn't understand but was always patient about what she called Faro's dour Calvinist reception of some of her more outrageous friends. The truth, he confessed, was that they made him nervous.

'Nervous, not you of all people, Faro,' she laughed.

Then one day as they toured the exhibits at yet another gallery opening, she realised that he wasn't listening. Instead he was staring transfixed by the painting of a smiling young woman, rich blue satin draped over one seductively bare shoulder, her face turned coquettishly towards them.

'Faro—you haven't heard a word.'

Then as Imogen stared into his face she was taken aback by his expression. Desire, lust— natural enough in a man, but this was different. As if the gates of hell had opened, she thought afterwards, little guessing that for Jeremy Faro they had indeed opened and shoved him down a path into a nightmare of events, ghosts he thought laid for ever, never to confront again in his mortal life.

'Gorgeous, isn't she?' Imogen said lamely, squinting at the name, *Portrait of Lena*.

Faro nodded, said slowly. 'Lena. Lena Hamilton.'

'And by Rossetti too.' Imogen smiled. 'A Pre-Raphaelite.'

'It is indeed,' Faro replied.

'You knew her?' Imogen demanded sharply.

Again Faro nodded.

Imogen turned to the portrait. 'Scotch, is she? I thought you never came to London.'

Ignoring that, he said, 'She is—or was—from Glasgow.'

Imogen took his arm. 'Tell me more, Faro. I'm intrigued, how did you come to meet her?'

'Imogen, darling—oh, there you are!'

The interruption came across the crowded floor as Olivia, Faro's stepdaughter-in-law, rushed towards them.

The two women embraced and Olivia planted a kiss on his cheek.

'Vince not with you?' Faro asked.

'An emergency—at the palace.' Vince was a junior physician to Her Majesty's Household and such emergencies were common among the hordes of young royals.

Olivia grinned. 'The usual story, not that he's bothered. You know what he's like, doesn't care for these grand occasions—took that from you, Stepfather, badly brought up,' she laughed. 'Count van Schütz is dying to meet you, Imo, he's read one of your books. Will you excuse us, Stepfather?'

She didn't get an answer and Imogen darted Faro a look of concern as she was led away.

He wanted very much to be alone at that moment. His heart was beating wildly. He could hear it and in that atmosphere of heat, expensive cigar smoke and heady perfumes, he hoped that he wasn't going to collapse, make an exhibition of himself and embarrass Olivia and Imogen, as the portrait of Lena refused to release him, holding him hypnotised as her smiling eyes had once held him more than thirty years ago.

The gate to hell had indeed opened. There was no escape, the world of 1887 had dissolved, had never been born and 27-year-old Jeremy Faro was in Kent.

The nightmare was about to begin.

CHAPTER ONE

1860

Constable Jeremy Faro was in pursuit of a notorious criminal who had made his escape over the border. This villain was a man of many disguises with as many crimes, including murder, to his name and only Faro had ever seen him face to face. In the fight that followed, beaten to the ground and left for dead, he survived his injuries with one important fact to offer.

He would recognise Macheath again.

'We have had one piece of luck, Constable,' said Detective Sergeant Noble, recently seconded from the Glasgow police. 'He is down in Kent, at present held in custody at Abbey Wood. So you had better get down there sharpish and bring him back to stand trial. You are the only witness who can identify him.'

Faro had little option in the matter, despite misgivings that he refrained from outlining. He knew his enemy and, more importantly, that all the restraint that the Kent police had on offer might be totally inadequate to detain this wily character in one of their cells. In addition, an added complication apparently unnoted by DS Noble, Faro realised that the

Macheath he had encountered could be completely transformed by shaving off his beard.

But an order from above was a command and there were hints of promotion in store. Young Constable Faro was proving competent and trustworthy, and the success of this assignment carried with it hints of promotion. His remarkable powers of observation and deduction in solving baffling cases had already much impressed Chief Inspector McFie, recently retired. These were, however, somewhat cynically regarded by DS Noble, who showed a regrettable tendency to throw all the impossible jobs his way and make them sound deceptively simple. And tracking down Macheath on a very inadequate description fitted this category extremely well.

*   *   *

Faro loved trains and leaving Edinburgh behind brought a great sense of excitement whatever awaited him at the end of his journey. Fascinated by what was still the novelty and daring of travel by railway, this would be his first visit to England as he had never been further south than the Scottish Borders.

Taking his seat in an empty compartment as the train steamed out of Waverley Station, he relaxed and stared out of the window determined to enjoy the outward journey in this good spell of early autumn weather with its dramatic glimpses of changing colours.

He determinedly thrust aside gloomy presentiments about the future since neither DS Noble, nor anyone else for that matter, had advised him how he was expected to accomplish his return journey on a London train bound for Edinburgh, armed only with a set of handcuffs to restrain a wily criminal and murderer whose attempts at escape had been remarkably successful so far.

As what lay ahead was for him a foreign territory as well as one that predictably involved pursuit of his quarry, to be well read was also to be well armed, so he had purchased a guidebook and a map for the journey—he had a particular fondness for maps—to acquaint himself as much as possible with the south of England.

He read that the area in which he was to be involved, between Deptford and Dartford, was poor and ugly and in the Twenties, according to social commentator William Cobbett, 'such ugliness received a considerable addition by the sticking up of some shabby genteel houses surrounded with dead fences and things called gardens. Together bricks and sticks proclaimed "Here dwell vanity and poverty".'

Laying aside the guidebook, he stared out of the window. Certainly as they left Northumberland and Yorkshire behind, the countryside that the train steamed through was beyond any in his experience, mostly flat and occasionally undulating, like some vast deserted meadowland stretching to the horizons, intersected by tiny hamlets, green trees, farm animals and the occasional mansion house of a great estate.

The approach to the industrial towns filled the sky with their smoking chimneys, a glimpse of narrow streets and mean hovels, overshadowed by the smoking monsters of Blake's 'dark Satanic mills'. Reaching London at last he was delighted to find the North Kent railway line led directly to Abbey Wood eight miles distant. As he changed trains, the final descent into the lush greenery of the countryside made him sigh with relief, a feeling that was to be short-lived. He was not completely surprised at the end of that long train journey to be met at the local police station, no more than a cottage in the village street, by a flurry of activity, apologies, red faces all round and considerable embarrassment. He was a day too late. The pathetically inadequate prison cell might have struck terror into the heart of a local poacher or a disruptive drunk but was never intended to house a dangerous criminal, and his quarry had found little difficulty in making his escape by wrenching out two very insecure iron bars on the window.

Sergeant Wilson was suitably apologetic for

4

his wasted journey. 'We understand that yesterday night he entered Brettle Manor, three miles distant down the road at Bexleyheath, broke a window and stole some food from the pantry. As there was nothing else taken, it looks as if this was a survival burglary only. Here are the details, Constable.'

Faro took the sheet of paper and sighed deeply. He would interview the owner but had scant hope of any clues. Macheath and his lunch would be miles away. It now remained his painful duty to telegraph Edinburgh and acquaint DS Noble with this dire news, showing remarkable restraint in respectfully not adding: I told you so.

While awaiting a reply, hopeful that it would be for his immediate return journey to Edinburgh, Faro's hunger was appeased by mutton pies washed down with the excellent local ale. The constables beamed on him, so relieved to find a decent sort of chap who, after travelling all that way, understood their predicament regarding the escaped prisoner and took it all so calmly.

Not so DS Noble, alas. Never the most patient of men, his telegraph in return was made to sound almost as if Faro had been personally responsible for this calamity. As he read the words, he could almost hear that roar of anger and frustration.

'Do not return to Edinburgh until quarry found. Our last chance to recapture. That is an order.'

When the red faces had subsided a little, Sergeant Wilson said, 'You'd better prepare for a long stay, mate. The local alehouse will give you a room.' He was sorry to depress Faro but felt it his duty to add, 'Like as not your villain headed for London. He could hide there for ever and a day.'

This dismal prophecy echoed Faro's own feelings on the matter.

Exasperated at the prospect of a trail gone cold and a fruitless local search with few clues to follow, he began walking briskly along the village street towards Bexleyheath, three miles distant, when he was hailed by a once familiar voice.

'Hello there, Jeremy!'

The man who rushed across from the direction of the railway station, carrying what looked like a roll of canvas under his arm, belonged to his far distant Orkney schooldays.

'Erland Flett. What on earth are you doing here?'

'I might ask the same thing,' Erland chuckled. 'Were you on that train by any chance? I was just collecting this parcel from the luggage van.' Frowning, he looked Faro up and down and grinned. 'Well, well, I heard you were in the police. In Edinburgh. What brings you down to England's green and pleasant land?'

'Just police business,' Faro replied.

6

'No uniform?'

Faro shook his head. 'No. For obvious reasons.' And without further explanation: 'Just here for a few days,' he added, more in forlorn hope than certainty. 'And yourself?'

'Still painting. I expect you've heard of the Pre-Raphaelite Brotherhood even in Edinburgh. Well, I'm staying with William Morris.' He grinned. 'Topsy, we call him, on account of his mop of curls. Red House is just a short distance away, fairly newly built and although I'm a watercolourist, he asked me to help out on some of the extensive decor, murals and so forth.' And suddenly excited, 'Where are you staying?'

'I've just arrived.' When he mentioned the local alehouse, Erland shook his head violently.

'No, no, that won't do at all. You must come back with me—and stay at Red House.'

'Where's Red House?'

'At Bexleyheath.'

'That's a coincidence—I have to see someone at—' and consulting the note, Faro said, 'at Brettle Manor.'

'They're almost our next-door neighbours.' Erland grinned. 'We'll soon arrange that for you. Come on, that's settled then—'

Cutting short his protests, Erland went on, 'I insist. You'll be made most welcome, accepted as my guest. And you'll love it. It's a free house, painters, their models, their families all drift in and out. Gabriel Rossetti, Burne-Jones, Ford Madox Brown—they are here almost all the time.' Pausing he frowned and asked wistfully, 'Do you paint, by any chance?'

'I once tackled the front door at home.'

Erland shook his head. 'Don't mean that kind. Thought being a watercolourist might be included in your many talents.'

' 'Fraid not. Can't even draw a straight line. And where did you get that "many talents" from?'

'You were so good at school. At everything. Remember?' And Erland pointed across the road to an alehouse. 'Look, let's go in there. It's not much but we can have a pint of porter and a pie, chance to catch up on things while we wait for the Morris wagonette. Collecting me in half an hour. Still have my game leg, you know,' he added cheerfully.

Faro had already noticed the slight limp, the game leg that was in fact a club foot. In addition Erland had suffered from fainting fits, what the Orcadians called 'doon-fallin' sickness'.

As for that school friendship, tall and strong and ready with his fists, Faro had defended the smaller, lame, white-faced boy against his tormentors. From that first day Erland had looked upon him as his saviour and as the Fletts and Faros were distantly related to each other, as were almost every family in Orkney, he proudly claimed Jeremy as close kin.

8

The ale served them at the rickety table was acceptable, and Faro insisted that he had already eaten, but the dismal surroundings were not impressive nor was the prospect of hospitality at all promising. It suggested that Faro would be wise to consider his extreme good fortune in finding a more comfortable lodging near the site of his investigation.

Erland leant forward and said excitedly, 'Having you here is the most marvellous coincidence. You'll never guess what? My great news is that I'm about to be married. Next week. And you can be my best man. My best friend at school and my cousin! What could be more appropriate? Are you married yet?'

'Not quite. But I have a young lady.'

'Oooh.' Erland leant forward, laughing delightedly. 'Your intended! Tell me all about her.'

Faro was grateful that the arrival of one of the Red House grooms saved an explanation to Erland of the sensitive domestic situation he had left in Edinburgh, the one fly in the ointment so to speak. The young woman he was keeping company with, Lizzie Spark, had an illegitimate son Vince, aged twelve, who hated him.

As they left the alehouse, waiting outside was the most extraordinary conveyance Faro had ever encountered. There was certainly nothing in Edinburgh to equal the horse-drawn coach with curtains made of leather and a canvas, chintz-lined canopy. Erland explained that it had been specially built at Morris's instruction by Philip Webb, the designer of Red House. Faro wondered what passers-by thought of this relic from another age that bore a weird resemblance to something from a medieval tapestry. As it swayed and pulled up the hill to swing along the road, Erland pointed out a few labourers' cottages built from the remains of the Augustinian priory suppressed during the reign of King Henry VIII.

Thin plumes of smoke rising into the clear air indicated Upton, which Erland explained, as its name suggested, was an upper or higher settlement within the large parish of Bexley with ninety-seven dwellings, homes to farm workers, gardeners, carriers, plus an alehouse, the Royal Oak.

The approach suggested an early development of suburban villas, the march of bricks and mortar over the fields of Bexley as London's population sprawled ever outwards.

Later he read in his guidebook that by the Thirties Bexley's new town was growing in popularity with more than 2000 inhabitants and ten years later the vicar instigated the building of a new chapel close to Watling Street for his parishioners. Soon afterwards the railways arrived: one line running through Bexley via Lewisham and another further north through Woolwich.

As they entered the village street, Faro begged to be excused, saying that he must first call at the local police station, which Erland pointed out was conveniently, or inconveniently for the criminally minded, almost directly opposite the alehouse.

He thanked the groom, saying that he would walk the rest of the way, but Erland would have none of it.

'We will wait for you,' he said cheerfully. 'There is no hurry.'

That this was a peaceful community was indicated by the fact that there was no constable in evidence in response to the bell on the counter.

Returning to the wagonette, Erland laughed at his stern expression.

'No one there, eh? My dear old chap, the explanation is perfectly obvious. Not at all unusual. This is a haven of peace and as so little crime is anticipated, Constable Muir is either out after the local poacher or at home having his supper. And having come all this way, surely your business can wait until tomorrow morning.'

As they approached their destination, Erland pointed out Brettle Manor, on the east side of Red House.

Faro was immediately interested, and as the wagonette lacked windows, he slid along the leather curtain and stuck his head out for a closer look, to see a thin thread of smoke

11

drifting skywards from a decrepit thatched cottage. Almost hidden by an overgrown garden of hedgerows and trees, it was very much at odds with this area of neat suburbia encountered thus far.

Bewildered, he turned to Erland: 'Brettle Manor?'

Erland laughed. 'No! You can't see it from this angle. That is Hope Cottage on the edge of the Brettle estate—belongs to a wily old devil who refused to sell out to Sir Philip. The manor is in fact a new villa built just before Red House, carved out from the original orchards.'

A short distance and a long wall followed. 'There's the manor now. Near neighbours. Not long now.'

Craning his neck, Faro glimpsed a projecting porch flanked by square window bays as, with a gesture to take in the countryside, Erland continued, 'Once this heath was pitted by sand and gravel diggings traversed by Watling Street, the old Roman road linking London, Canterbury and Dover and in the last century it was the wild haunt of footpads.

'Red House stands on what was the pilgrims' road to Canterbury, a fact dear to Topsy's heart, a devoted Chaucerian. Such a romantic, he fell in love with the medieval ruins of Lesnes Abbey and Hall Place, the old Tudor mansion over yonder.' And a confidential whisper, 'Built a couple of years ago and cost a small fortune, don't you know, £4000—'

A fortune indeed and an almost unimaginable amount of money to an Edinburgh policeman, thought Faro, as Erland went on:

'Morris is rich, of course, but he couldn't afford a country estate and Red House was over five times his annual income from his father's legacy. But newly married, you know, he wanted a new house. Ah, we are nearly there.' He laughed. 'And his great friend, Dante Gabriel Rossetti was delighted to hear that his friend Topsy had chosen to build on a place known as Hog's Hole.'

Suddenly the wagonette swung and swayed through the gate of a high wall.

'Home at last!' said Erland. 'Welcome to Morris's "Earthly Paradise"!'

CHAPTER TWO

The first sight of Red House gave Faro a feeling of astonished pleasure to see a building so vividly picturesque and uniquely original, startling in red brick, an unusual colour for one used to the grey stones of Scotland. An immense, red-tiled, steep roof, a gable shaped like a giant pepper pot and high, small-paned medieval windows suggested the house of a religious community rather than an artist's

13

domestic residence.

As they approached the low, wide porch with its massive oak door, Erland chuckled. 'This is called the Pilgrim's Rest. Appropriate, don't you think?'

Stepping out of the wagonette Faro paused, breathing in the thin fresh air, welcomed by sweet garden smells of apples from the gnarled old fruit trees glimpsed over the orchard walls.

The tall figure of a girl standing in the porch disappeared inside.

'That's Janey, Topsy's wife,' Erland whispered. 'I'll introduce you and she'll soon find a room for you.'

Already somewhat apprehensive at the prospect of encountering professional and famous artists, a strata of society of which his life in Edinburgh and Orkney had offered no experience, Jeremy, following Erland into the now empty hall, put a hand on his arm and whispered:

'I have only one request. No word that I'm a policeman. Keep that to yourself, if you please.'

Erland laughed. 'Your secret is safe with me. I have no intention of giving the game away, old chap. A policeman in their midst would cast a definite blight on their behaviour—that is, of course, until they get to know you,' he added hastily. And with an apologetic cough, 'You will have to get used to it, ignoring things, I mean. Some of them behave a little odd. A law unto themselves, as we say. Use laudanum and chloral, as well as opium, not just for health reasons, to keep minor aches and pains at bay, but just to keep their spirits up.'

'Do you?' Faro demanded.

In answer, Erland shrugged and then, looking anxiously at Faro's expression, he said: 'You know what I mean, I'm sure. After all, artists often need this sort of stimulant, Rossetti in particular. And of course the wine flows continually. I'm sure you won't judge them. They mean no harm, they're decent, good souls.'

Harm or no, and with hopes of a dram of whisky after his travels fast disappearing, Faro decided it was none of his business. He must temporarily forget his Calvinist upbringing and the law's rulings on illegal drugs, and assuring Erland he understood perfectly, he cut short his own misgivings.

As well as being a splendid location and certainly more comfortable than the brief glimpse suggested the local alehouse might have on offer, whatever went on in Red House, he was prepared to ignore. This impromptu visit was only for a few days. An interesting experience for the beginning of his investigation, an investigation which he was under orders to conscientiously follow, although he guessed that Macheath would be far from Kent by now, with London fairly accessible.

15

Erland went in search of Janey Morris and he had a chance to take in his surroundings, the wide entrance hall through the porch with its red flagged floor and unpainted woodwork, plain, well lit, but quite ordinary, not at all what he had expected from the exterior, with high windows excluding any views of the gardens.

Gazing up the handsome oak staircase with its extended newel posts, used to the overblown clutter of present-day domestic architecture, he recognised that this more closely resembled the earlier Georgian age, for there were no cornices, no mouldings, no ornamentation, just plain skirting boards.

The exterior had suggested a religious community but the interior, with its sturdy simplicity, would have done credit to a village school or a country parsonage. There was more to it. This tall turreted house, plain and functional, was also playful with an amalgam of surprises: in the absence of conventional decoration inside there were small arches showing sills and sash windows of all shapes, little casements of a size to shoot an arrow through, the kind of imaginative home a child would love.

Awaiting Erland's return he strolled back to the open door and realised that this was also a place for knights of old. That inner courtyard with its well house like a giant candle-snuffer suggested a departure point for long-forgotten battles and crusades.

Gazing upwards at the great tiled barn-like roof with weathervane and turret to the fountain splashing up just yards away, again he felt that he had set foot in a foreign land, a time of legend and fairy tale. Although Edinburgh had more than its share of Gothic architecture, mostly devoted to church buildings, there were few models for architects to use for the smaller detached domestic dwellings which the new affluent society demanded.

Back in that inner porch of welcome he looked up at the exposed roof beams and trusses, as well as some brick arches, forming external features brought indoors and asymmetrically positioned.

He was to discover that Philip Webb's creation had been designed not as a vertical London townhouse nor a stuccoed suburban villa but a house commodious but not grand, handsome but not flashy, medieval in spirit but modern in function with family rooms for a clutch of children, as befitted the newly married William and Jane. There were also guest rooms, servants quarters and a studio. An artist's house and a gentleman's residence.

He wandered into an open room with a huge fireplace and a wide shallow grate, its scaled-down medieval shape including a hood but lacking a mantelpiece.

Footsteps! Erland had returned. 'So this is

17

where you are. Isn't it magnificent? Gabriel describes it as more a poem than a house. Nothing like it in dear old Orkney—or in Scotland,' he added proudly.

Faro nodded in agreement as Erland went on, 'Janey is rather busy at the moment. She told me to show you to your room.'

Faro hesitated. 'Are you sure this is all right?'

'Of course it is all right, old chap. You are most welcome. You'll meet Janey and Topsy and the others at dinner.' Turning as Faro followed him upstairs, he said, 'Well, what do you think?'

'I'm most impressed.'

As they reached the landing Erland indicated a small arch. 'This way. Mind your head, it wasn't intended for anyone as tall as you. Topsy is quite short, you know—like me.'

As he threw open a door across a wide floor, Faro glimpsed a postered bed, almost the sole furnishing in a room with high, narrow, arched windows.

'You'll be happy here, Jeremy, mark my words. This place is magic. Pure magic. Make yourself at home, I will see you shortly.'

Glancing around, Faro considered his good fortune. He could believe Erland; this place was magic.

But magic had another darker side. However there was no indication of what the future held as he took in his surroundings, the prospect of a pleasant and completely unique adventure,

Red House near enough to the local police office to keep in constant touch for news. Though what he was expected to do he was not quite sure until someone sighted Macheath. Of that, Faro had little hope and unless matters moved at an alarming speed, which a brief experience of the local police at Abbey Wood did not suggest was at all likely, he would be here for Erland's wedding.

Unpacking his valise, he sat down at the small table and brought up to date his logbook, which would be required as evidence of his investigation. The task completed, laying it aside, he decided this might be a great adventure after all. He was unlikely to ever be in Kent again or to have the opportunity to meet a group of famous artists once he returned to the everyday duties of an Edinburgh policeman.

An experience indeed. As for Orkney—by comparison with Edinburgh, how dull the simple life his family had enjoyed for generations must have seemed before his father made the momentous break from tradition, joining the Edinburgh City Police, only to be killed by a runaway cab while on duty. An accident that his mother flatly refused to accept, certain that he had been deliberately run down, a fact that, in a life still far in the future, was to be one of Chief Inspector Jeremy Faro's greatest cases.

A tap on the door announced Erland's

return. 'Supper will be ready soon. What do you think of your room?' Bouncing on the bed he smiled. 'It is so good to see you again. I still can't believe my luck. Amazing, isn't it—that we are both to be married soon. You did mention a young lady, tell me about her.'

So Faro told him all about Lizzie and Vince, watching his friend's face anxiously as he spoke. Not that he was ashamed of Lizzie, despite the fact that she was regarded as a social outcast because of her illegitimate child. Faro was intensely proud of the way she had overcome adversity and had borne and lovingly reared this child, the result of rape by a visiting guest one summer while she was employed as a maid in a big house.

From Edinburgh she could expect no sympathy or help, only contempt and condemnation. In many cases, girls less fortunate than Lizzie had their babies torn from their arms and thrust into workhouses until they were old enough for slave labour while their unfortunate young mothers often spent the rest of their days in asylums for the insane.

Such appalling treatment Faro found difficult to forgive in a society that he was dedicated to protect, seeing so much of the lowlife of the higher echelons, the guardians of Edinburgh society emerging from brothels on his beat in Leith Walk. These were the very men who had disgraced and ruined his poor

Lizzie.

At the end of his story, Erland nodded vigorously. 'Don't you worry, old chap, don't give it another thought. The fellows here will be entirely on your side. They consider it a noble duty to rescue unfortunate women and give them status and education.'

Enthusiastically he went on to quote examples of the Pre-Raphaelites who had taken girls from humble backgrounds as models and elevated them to higher ranks, even marrying them. Models such as Rossetti's new bride, Elizabeth Siddal, another Lizzie, who had been seen working in a milliner's shop, and Janey Morris, daughter of a stableman and a laundress, living in a backyard hovel in Oxford, kept out of society for two years while Morris educated her before they married, much to his upper-class mother's disapproval.

'What of your Lena?' Faro asked.

Erland laughed. 'Oh, she's well off, grandfather a rich Glasgow merchant.'

Asked how they met, Erland smiled. 'So romantic, old chap. Quite by accident—or fate as you wish—on a train journey. An orphan, from Glasgow, lost her parents when she was quite young, she had been living with an aunt who had died recently. I helped her with her luggage. She had missed her train, and was in quite a state.

'I was meeting Topsy Morris and Rossetti,

who took one look at her and insisted she had a meal with us. As we talked, we learnt that she was a seamstress and had considered going to London in search of work perhaps as an embroideress but had no idea of where to begin looking for employment. As well as being a stunner, as they call lovely girls here,' he paused to sigh and close his eyes, 'she was quite beautiful and I could see Gabriel watching her, narrow-eyed, surveying her as he does prospective models, already positioning them in some of his Arthurian paintings.

'Janey—who you'll be meeting—and Burne-Jones's wife, Georgie, are great embroiderers. Well, over that meal we shared, I guessed how nervous Lena was about going to London. At a crossroads, she didn't want to return to Glasgow either and it was as if I could see into Topsy and Gabriel's minds at that moment. I knew exactly what they were going to say. She was to come back to Red House. There was plenty of employment there for a seamstress or an embroideress.'

Erland laughed. 'Oh, it was so wonderful, as if Divine Providence had stepped in. At that time I must admit I had little hope; Gabriel Rossetti so handsome—all his models fall in love with him, although he was officially engaged to his Lizzie for several years before they got married. That was a bit of a heartbreak for her, knowing he's not the faithful type and she's past thirty.

22

'Anyway, I was wrong about Lena, I soon found out that although she loved modelling for him—he said she was one of his best, so serene, she could sit quite immobile for hours on end, so very still—I thought her face always lit up when she saw me. At first I told myself it was only because she was grateful to me for introducing her to the artistic community here—I didn't dare hope for more than that.'

Pausing, he frowned. 'I couldn't believe that she was in love with me—how could any woman find me attractive by comparison with these men of genius—yet she wanted to marry me—be my wife.'

He looked astonished and shook his head. 'I have to confess to you, old chap, since we are old friends and cousins, that although we are to be married in a few days, we have—well, er, my lovely Lena is already my wife in everything but the marriage ceremony,' he added proudly. 'Not that such matters are regarded as important here. Jeremy, I am the luckiest man in the whole world for soon we will be together for ever, till death us do part. Wait till you meet her, see if you don't agree with me. Everyone loves her.'

A bell sounded. 'That's dinner now.'

Faro set aside his frustration at failing to contact the local constable. Evening would be too late to call on Brettle Manor—without his uniform. Besides, he told his conscience, the trail for Macheath in Upton had almost

23

certainly gone cold.

CHAPTER THREE

As they assembled in the dining room Faro decided this was as remote in its setting from any table he had ever supped at and, looking at the painted walls and ceiling, he doubted if there was one to match it in the rest of Britain.

The centre of the large room was held by a great round table and huge armchairs straight from the *Tales of King Arthur and His Knights* and the company were in keeping with their setting. The ladies in rich medieval gowns, vividly coloured, looked as if they might have stepped from the murals painted on the walls, for which they had doubtless modelled.

All took their seats and awaited the arrival of their host, William Morris, who to Faro's astonishment was wearing a suit of mail and a helmet complete with visor.

Erland whispered that Morris had ordered it for one of his paintings and it had just arrived. Trying it on he liked it so much he was giving it an airing. Everyone seemed to like it too, and his choice was applauded. Faro, looking round, felt the scene at the dining table was one of their paintings personified, lacking only a title from some medieval romance. William Morris and Dante Gabriel Rossetti, bearded, both

24

comfortably rounded and neither as tall as himself, suggested that, like their ladies, they might have stepped down from some painting, in their case the background of some early saint's martyrdom.

Erland rose and introduced him to the assembled group, saying this was his cousin from Orkney. Rossetti immediately responded, stretching a hand across the table.

'Dear chap, you are most welcome.' And to Erland, 'Did your cousin come direct and, if so, where is his dragon ship? I demand we see it and I trust we have found room for it.'

Everyone laughed and Erland looked bewildered as the men roared with mirth and Rossetti said, 'Congratulations, Erland dear fellow. Don't you know you have brought a Viking into our midst. Most acceptable. Don't you agree, Topsy old chap?'

Morris chuckled. 'I do indeed. Put a horned helmet on him—see if we have one somewhere, Gabriel—and he would look the part.'

Their reflections in the large mirrors showed Erland and the new man, Jeremy Faro, were a complete contrast. Faro was tall and slim with thick fair hair and dark eyebrows over deep-set, dark-blue, strangely watchful eyes. With the keen eye of the artist, Rossetti noticed the high cheekbones, long straight nose, and that sensual wide-lipped mouth, vulnerable in such a stern face, suggesting warmth, tenderness and even passion, unconcealed as it was by the fashion for facial hair run riot. Rossetti decided that, according to the Orkney legends, Erland belonged to the short dark-haired hunters who had built the mysterious brochs and the early cairns while Faro's forebears, the tall, fair Viking invaders, had come many centuries later.

And Rossetti, who knew a lot more about human nature than most, shrewdly guessed that as a schoolboy in Kirkwall, Erland's stammer and slight limp had made him the target of cruel torments and mimicry from other boys and that Faro had fought many a battle on his behalf, thereby winning his undying devotion.

Rossetti could not know that the story went further. When later the village girls in Orkney gravitated to handsome Jeremy, he did not seem to notice what was on offer, the one exception being Inga St Ola, the strange wild girl who was his constant companion. But his dreams and ambitions were to leave Orkney to follow his policeman father over to the mainland—to Scotland and the Edinburgh Police Force. Aware of the frailty of human hearts, where beauty was often all where love was concerned, Rossetti could well imagine that Faro had tried to direct the flutter of eager females in his friend Erland's direction—without success.

The truth was that women of all ages had

always found Jeremy Faro dynamic and, even in his short time in Edinburgh, he chose to ignore appraising glances from young females. He could not know how Erland had envied him, wistful that his friend could so easily find love if he wanted it, love that he had sought in vain until Lena, that miracle of his life, came along.

Now Gabriel Rossetti clapped his hands and, rising from the table, walked round and treated Faro to an inspection. 'You're right, we must find a painting to have him model for us. What have we—something suitably historical from those islands at the World's End.'

'Excellent, oh excellent.' Morris leant over the table. 'Tell us about yourself. Is it true what Erland says about seal people—selkies, they call them in Orkney?'

Faro smiled assent; his own grandmother was believed to be a selkie and she had webbed fingers and toes. But he decided not to mention that, conscious of the uproar such a bizarre fact would arouse.

'There must be legends, Tops, something we might use as a backdrop to one of our paintings,' said Rossetti frowning.

This became the topic of eager discussion between the two while Faro looked on. No one had asked him what brought him to Edinburgh from Orkney or, even more importantly, what he was doing in the south of England or even how long he intended to stay.

Whatever their reasons, that no direct questions were asked was a considerable relief. He was not a very good liar and he realised that his ancestry was of much greater interest than his present state, the relationship Erland claimed and that imminent wedding, taken for granted no doubt as the reason for his being brought to stay under the roof of Red House.

And all the time they talked, the wine flowed, his glass never allowed to be more than half empty. This would never do, he told himself sternly, endeavouring to evade the bottles being passed round the table. Ale was the common drink and an occasional dram of whisky, but, unaccustomed to imbibing vast quantities of rich wines, he soon realised that he must exercise some restraint or he would not only be at the table but very shortly under it.

He observed that the ladies too indulged freely in the wine. Elizabeth Siddal, an ethereal creature with a cloud of golden hair that did not mask a vaguely unhappy and nervous expression. Janey Morris, tall, thin and gaunt, as dark as Elizabeth was fair, two wild-haired exotic creatures very different indeed to Edinburgh matrons and living depictions of paintings around them. Only Georgina 'Georgie' Burne-Jones paled very slightly by comparison.

Erland's Lena was absent. Where was she, Gabriel demanded, and Erland said that she had gone to London, shopping with one of the other models, Poppy, for clothes for the wedding and material for their embroidered tapestries.

'What a seamstress she is, an absolute treasure. And a great model. One of the best ever, isn't that so, Tops?' said Gabriel. 'I've already put her into one of my paintings as Mary Magdalene at the Empty Sepulchre. Wait till you see it.'

*   *   *

Next morning, Faro, conscious of an acute headache and wishing he had not drunk quite so much wine at supper, was glad of a bracing walk in the fresh air and a duty visit to the police station. The door was open but the office devoid of Constable Muir once more. He scribbled a note and made his exit, witnessed by an ancient, bewhiskered man leaning heavily on a stick.

Staring up at him from under the brim of an equally ancient hat, he chuckled. 'You must be a stranger here, mister. Constable's out on his beat, never at the station afore ten. Is there owt I can do for thee? Folk call me Jim Boone. Live over yonder—Hope Cottage, can't miss it.'

Declining the kind offer, clearly to his informant's disappointment, who Faro felt would have enjoyed a deeper acquaintance, he headed towards Brettle Manor reflecting on the dismal prospects if ever serious crime should descend on the village.

A tree-lined drive gave way to a substantial but considerably less imposing villa than Red House and walking up to the front door he rang the doorbell vigorously. There was no reply.

A search led to the back premises. As he approached the kitchen door, he noticed again the tiny thread of smoke some distance from the house, now revealed as the ruinous cottage he had observed from the wagonette, stoutly fenced off from the rest of the Brettle estate, the much disputed home of the ancient gentleman he had just encountered.

As decrepit as its owner, with thatched roof sagging, tiny garden a defiant wilderness of weeds, it certainly did no credit to the handsome house at whose kitchen door he awaited some response.

At last his summons conjured up Mrs Lunn the housekeeper, large, red-faced and distinctly hostile, drying her hands on an apron and demanding to know what he wanted and she wasn't buying anything.

Asking politely for the owner of the house, he was informed that sir and madam were not at home and, regarding him suspiciously, what was his business anyway. 'I am here in connection with the recent break-in,' he said, producing his official note of authority.

Hands on hips, evading his eyes, she swept it aside. 'Is that so now? Who told you about it, I might ask.'

'I am a policeman, madam, and I suggest you read that.'

'You don't look much like a policeman— where's your uniform?' she demanded suspiciously.

'Read the note, if you please,' he said sternly.

With a reluctant sigh she did so and wearily stepped aside to allow him into the kitchen. Asked to detail the events of the burglary, she did so with some reluctance, on the grounds that the local constable knew them already, had been here several times and made notes which he could read at the station.

'This is just wasting my time,' she said shortly. 'Once again, all I could tell them—and now you—is that I came down that morning at six-thirty as usual to find the window broken. When sir and madam are abroad, the safety of the house is my responsibility. Last thing at night before retiring, I check that all doors and windows are locked, also the one over there,' she pointed, 'leading into the main rooms of the house. As that hadn't been tampered with, it must have upset the thief, so he just took some bread and cheese and a bottle of wine from the pantry. That was all. Hardly worth all the fuss—calling the police and so forth . . .'

Walking round the kitchen, Faro observed little beyond a rack of outdoor clothes on the

31

door but he was conscious of her nervous gaze following him.

As he examined the window she sighed.

'No use you doing that now. The police came that very morning afterwards and inspected everything.'

'And they were satisfied that the contents of the house were intact.'

'Of course they were. As I've already told you, I had to unlock the connecting door to get into my kitchen. There was no way a thief could get into the rest of the house,' she said shortly.

'Except by the front door, of course.'

She gave an indignant sniff. 'Impossible. Never opened. Barred and bolted while sir and madam are absent.'

'What about the window here—it was broken, you said?'

'That was repaired the same day by the handyman.'

'Does he live on the premises?'

'Of course not. He's lives in the village.'

'His address, please.'

'What on earth do you want that for?' Mrs Lunn demanded suspiciously as he wrote it down.

Faro pretended not to hear and asked, 'Are there any other staff I can talk to?'

'Of course not,' was the indignant reply. 'I am in sole charge while sir and madam are away.'

'No housemaids?'

Mrs Lunn hesitated. 'A lass from nearby, but her services aren't needed at present.'

'The cottage in the garden?'

'That is no concern of ours.' Mrs Lunn made a furious gesture. 'It is not in our garden either, and Jim Boone is just a wicked old devil—' and as Faro had already guessed—'his property a disgrace to this house and to sir and madam. He refused to sell it to them although it encroached on our property and he got the law on his side. It shouldn't be allowed, lowering the tone of the whole district, him and his mangy savage dog.'

Faro was silent, his sympathy with eccentric old people, defending the habitations where they had lived all their lives, as well as earlier generations. When the developing railways bisected the country or newcomers like the Brettles wished to move them on they were well within their moral rights for indignation and refusal to be put off or even bought off their land.

'Have you any suspicions why this thief should have broken in?'

'I have indeed. I think he was a vagrant, one of them gypsies that's always passing through the village, always on the scrounge.'

'Indeed. And had you seen any of the gypsies lurking about before the break-in?'

She shrugged. 'Might have done, but I can't remember exactly when. I wish now I had kept it to myself, felt it was my duty to tell the police anyway. Sir and madam would expect me to report things like that.'

'And you did right, Mrs Lunn.'

That pleased her. She said, 'Maybe they'll catch him red-handed next time.'

If the vagrant was, as he suspected, Macheath, there was small chance of that. The trail was cold; any clues had vanished under Mrs Lunn's meticulous housekeeping although her evasive manner hinted that she knew the thief's identity.

If that was so, then why bring the matter so conscientiously to the notice of the police?

She could have had the broken window repaired on some other excuse, not that he guessed the owners of Brettle Manor would have even noticed anything amiss in their kitchen premises. However, he would check with the local glazier whose details she had given so reluctantly.

At the door, unable to conceal her relief at his departure, she said suspiciously, 'You're not from these parts are you?'

When he replied, 'From Edinburgh,' her eyes widened in a look of fear.

'Oh, one of them,' she muttered closing the door sharply as if he might have two heads and leaving him wondering what her reaction would have been had he said, 'From Orkney.'

CHAPTER FOUR

Returning to the police station, he found Constable Muir reinstalled, emerging from behind a cloud of redolent tobacco smoke from his clay pipe, established at a desk with his feet up on the counter and a glass of ale at hand.

Bidding him good morning, Faro introduced himself by handing over the note of authority. The constable, a fat man, bursting out of his uniform, read it reluctantly. It hinted at unwelcome activity and, scratching a large perspiring bald head, he glanced up at this most unwelcome stranger sent to destroy his comfortable existence.

Sighing over the neatly written details of Faro's visit to Brettle Manor, he opened a drawer and produced the reports, which included the glazier's bill for repairing the broken window, and which tallied with his own interview on the morning after the break-in.

Faro glanced through them. All were signed Constable P Muir, Florence Lunn but the statement regarding the break-in was signed 'X' (Bess Tracy). The time was 8.30.

'The lass can't read or write,' Muir explained.

'I understood that it was Mrs Lunn who notified you of the break-in that she discovered at six-thirty.'

Muir shook his head. 'What gave you that idea? No, it was Bess Tracy. Maybe on Mrs Lunn's instructions, of course. Thinks a lot of herself—the grand lady being housekeeper to the gentry. But it was Bess who arrived at the house that morning and saw the broken window.'

Handing the reports back, Faro said, 'Then I will need to interview her. Her address, please.'

Muir stared at him and, scribbling a note, said, 'Here it is. Half a mile away, just off the main road. Her father's the miller. But you'll be wasting your time. We made a note of everything she had to say. It's all in those reports.'

He held out his hand for their return and pointed out rather huffily that he was sole occupant of the police station and in charge of any local investigations, despite Mrs Lunn's turn of phrase, which had indicated a whole police force on the case.

Faro's suggestions of opening up the investigation were met not only by scorn but by faint hostility. Was he hinting that Upton Police, as personified by Constable P Muir, did not know their job?

He left wearily, informing the constable firmly that he would report each morning. Meanwhile he was staying at Red House where he was to be informed immediately, at any hour, should there be any news of Macheath.

But he knew that there was little chance of a successful outcome. The trail was now cold indeed. Perhaps he had thought there might be some clues leading to Macheath at Brettle Manor. Instead it had been a waste of time, Mrs Lunn's and his own, and he could not bear to sit around and wait in that dull, smoke-filled office every day in the vain hope of his quarry being sighted in the neighbourhood.

Walking along the road in the direction of Mill Cottage, he had an even closer look at the disreputable old cottage on the Brettle's estate. However, he felt he could safely dismiss the old man as the pantry thief as well as deciding that Muir was probably right and that little would be gained from a meeting with the maid, Bess.

*   *   *

The mill straddled a fast-moving stream, the nearby cottage on the edge of a wood where trees were being felled with an agreeable smell of fresh shavings accompanying the sound of a saw at work.

He walked round to investigate and had to call 'Mr Tracy' twice before the man gave up, straightened his back and turned angrily.

'Mr Tracy?' A nod. 'I would like a word with Bess—your daughter, I believe.'

37

Tracy looked at him coldly. A sullen brutal face under the leather helmet, a coarse mouth and beetle-black eyes.

'She ain't here,' he said and picked up his saw again.

Faro was not to be dismissed. He went closer, stood over him and demanded, 'When will she be at home?'

'I ain't got a notion about that. Ain't seen her for a day or two.'

He did not sound in the least concerned.

Faro asked: 'When do you expect her to return?'

Tracy put down the saw. 'She comes and goes as she likes. No daughter of mine,' he added angrily. 'Just like her mother, the rotten sow. And going the same way.'

Here was a delicate domestic problem but Faro persisted. 'Have you any idea, then, where I might be able to contact her?'

Tracy looked him over. 'She likes a smart fellow now that she's got in with them at yon Red House. You'll be all right,' he added candidly with a leering glance. 'Try the gardeners first, they might be able to tell you.' And deliberately turning his back, he returned to his task as if Faro did not exist.

As he was walking round to the front of the cottage, the door opened. A woman looked out, stealthily beckoning to him.

'A minute, sir, if you please. Don't listen to him, sir,' she said in scared tones. 'He don't

38

know what he's talking about. Our Bess is a good girl and—' Looking beyond Faro, listening to the sound of sawing which continued, she whispered, 'I'm worried about her. She was going a message for me, just to get a loaf of bread but she never came back. He had hit her again and she was that upset. I don't know where she can have got to.'

The woman, pale, thin with wispy brown hair tied back in an untidy bun, looked ready to burst into tears. Faro noticed the bruise on her cheek which indicated more than any words that Bess was not the only victim and that both wife and daughter had reason to be afraid of the brutal miller.

'They've never got along, those two. My Bess is a sweet lass, so gentle and kind, sir. I'm scared that she's run away, but she'd never do that and not tell me.'

'Have you any relatives or friends she might be staying with?'

'We have no family. None of her friends can tell me anything. She usually meets with some lasses on a Saturday night but when I asked, they'd never seen her.' Another startled look beyond Faro, listening intently to the sounds outside. 'She had no money with her either, only two pence for the loaf of bread.' She put a hand on Faro's arm. 'I don't know who you are, sir, or what you want with my Bess, but you look kind.' She paused. 'Not in any trouble, is she, sir?'

'Not at all.' Should he say that he was a policeman? No, he decided against that. 'Mrs Lunn at Brettle Manor sent me—Bess works for her occasionally,' he added hoping this vague statement would be enough.

A look of relief passed over Mrs Tracy's face. It vanished rapidly when he asked, 'Does Bess have a young man?'

'Do you mean, is she courting? I wouldn't go so far as to say that, sir, but she said she'd met a nice respectable sort of chap, a gardener at Red House up the road. When she didn't meet the lasses, they thought she must have gone out with him instead and they weren't worried until I told them she hadn't been home. Three days is a long time, sir, without any word of her.'

If this was only a domestic incident, an angry tyrant of a father who assaulted his womenfolk, then it was not for him to investigate.

'Have you mentioned this to Constable Muir, by any chance?'

She shook her head. 'He—' nodding towards the sawing sound, she whispered, 'he would kill me if I did that.'

'Then I shall do it for you, Mrs Tracy. Constable Muir is very reliable and he will keep a lookout and make some discreet enquiries.'

Tearfully she thanked him and he left, deciding to make some discreet enquiries of

40

his own. The discrepancies between the two statements of Mrs Lunn and Bess regarding the break-in bothered him. Some instinct also told him that there was more to Brettle Manor and Mrs Lunn than had been immediately obvious. Her nervous manner while he looked round the kitchen for instance. What was she so anxious about? And why hadn't she told him that it was Bess Tracy who informed Constable Muir and she was one person that he should talk to. A small detail perhaps but it made him uneasy. Was there was something amiss, some sinister connection that had been overlooked regarding the immediate disappearance of the girl who had notified Constable Muir of the break-in at Brettle Manor? And unless the long arm of coincidence had nothing to do with that incident, he had a feeling in his bones that Macheath was at large again.

As for tracking him down, it was of little consolation telling his conscience that he had begun his investigation with scrupulous care strictly according to his superior officer's orders, obeyed so unwillingly on what he felt and now knew with certainty was a fool's errand.

Walking the short distance back, he was not at all satisfied with his morning's work. However, this was an errand which had a surprising outcome in turning out to be an unexpected holiday, with the pleasant prospect of attending Erland's wedding as well as the privilege of staying in the magnificent surroundings of Red House. With a sigh, he decided he had in fact good reason to be secretly grateful to DS Noble in far away Edinburgh Police Office.

The rain began as he made his way back and he rushed indoors to escape the heavy downpour. Obviously there would be no gardeners roaming the grounds in such weather and he had yet to work out a plan of approaching them on the subject of the missing girl without revealing his role as a policeman to the entire staff and occupants of Red House.

*   *   *

In the course of his daily visits to the police station, Faro was soon to discover that Constable Muir was far less concerned than he had presumed would be the case regarding the missing girl. In Muir's opinion, based on the few words with her mother, she had found herself a fancy man somewhere and taken off with him.

'Country matters, lad. You're not in the big city now. These things happen all the time. Lasses tired of living at home and working their fingers to the bone meet flashy chaps who promise them the earth. Bess has always spread herself about a bit. Ask any of the local lads, they'll soon tell you chapter and verse—if you really want to know.' And with a shake of his head, 'Don't you worry—she'll be back, right as rain—and no doubt in the family way—when her new man gets tired of her.'

Muir was curious about Red House. At last he had someone who had first-hand knowledge of its eccentric but famous inhabitants. Faro received many hints and nods and had questions to field concerning rumour and speculation drifting from the local alehouse and floating across the counters of local shops regarding exciting and perhaps slightly improper events that took place within its walls.

Most decidedly, Muir envied Constable Faro, who was exceptionally fortunate to have found such a lodging while officially on police duty. As for Faro, he was happy to be enveloped daily in a bewildering atmosphere that suggested everyone had just arrived or was on the point of departure. He was forever clambering over boxes and baskets with materials spilling out everywhere, books, paintbrushes, the smell of linseed oil and turpentine among canvases that fought for room over embroideries.

Erland's tiny room at the back of the house, which he called his studio, wasn't much better and Faro realised sadly that, although his friend was a good landscape painter, his expertise was merely that of a good copyist.

Erland Flett had none of the stardust that fate had sprinkled on the Pre-Raphaelites and sadly could never hope to reach the dizzy heights of popularity attained by Dante Gabriel Rossetti, or touch the splendours of Holman Hunt, Ford Madox Brown and Burne-Jones, the remaining members of the quintet who occasionally roared through William Morris's Red House.

No one talked to Faro apart from during meals in the dining room where all were genially assembled fortified by good food and plentiful wine. During other hours, however, all he received for his polite greeting was a vague nod, a perplexed stare if he bumped into any of them in room or staircase or corridor. Sometimes he felt as though he was invisible.

'You've been accepted,' was Erland's gleeful response to this state of affairs. 'Wait until you see Lena. I expect her back tomorrow. I've missed her—can't bear to be away from her. Hate sleeping alone—after that wedding we will be together for ever! Oh, how I long for next week,' he sighed. 'And before that—we're to have a pre-wedding celebration, a masked ball, arranged by Topsy.'

*　　*　　*

On the following day, Faro returned from yet another futile daily visit to Constable Muir who had been making, it seemed, a 'few enquiries among the customers' at the local alehouse about the missing Bess. He shook his head over Faro's persistence.

What on earth could he do? The girl would turn up, just wait and see. A lot of trouble over an everyday event.

Faro couldn't convince Muir that some instinct warned him that there was a link between Bess's disappearance and the mysterious atmosphere at Brettle Manor.

Another excuse must be found for a return visit. He left Muir's office once more, relieved to breathe in fresh air. Although he enjoyed a pipe himself, he was prepared to spend money on good tobacco and considered that whatever the Constable was using had extremely doubtful origins.

But what happened a few minutes later banished all thoughts of the fate of the miller's missing daughter right out of his mind.

As he reached the gate of Red House, Faro stood aside to allow the approaching wagonette access. Following it in, he saw Erland waiting. He was standing on the porch and rushed forward to greet the slender girl who alighted.

So this was his beloved Lena. Erland, wreathed in smiles, turned, saw him and waited, leading Lena forward to be introduced.

Faro stepped back in astonishment.

She was no stranger.

He had seen her before.

At the Edinburgh High Court three years ago in July 1857 where she had emerged from a murder trial, accused of poisoning her lover, walking free, set at liberty by a Not Proven verdict.

CHAPTER FIVE

Lena Hamilton she called herself now. Her name was Madeleine Smith, Hamilton the name of her maternal grandfather, the famous architect and mastermind of Glasgow's Royal Exchange and the Western Bank.

Faro had been given the special privilege of attending the trial by Chief Inspector McFie. Already impressed and assured of this remarkable young policeman's future, he was keen to have his protégé's assessment of what promised to be the trial of the century.

Whatever the jury, seduced by her youth and charm, might decide, Faro was sure that there had been a serious miscarriage of justice. As he listened to the evidence, he was certain that she was guilty of poisoning her lover Emile L'Angelier by putting arsenic in his cocoa and that only her youth—she was twenty-one years old—her beauty and her place in the echelons of Glasgow society had saved her from the gallows.

A young girl from a prosperous background, daughter of an eminent and respected architect, about to marry William Minnoch, a bachelor in his early thirties and a senior member of a firm of merchant importers, a man approved of by her parents, Madeleine Smith had apparently been seduced by a heartless womaniser.

Such were the implications of the evidence in her favour.

Who would credit that she could ever have been willingly the lover of a lowborn Frenchman? Everyone knew what Frenchmen were like, especially women. The men too had bad memories of the Napoleonic wars. No doubt about it, France was still regarded by most people as Britain's natural enemy.

L'Angelier, however, was only French by descent. His anti-monarchist family had fled from persecution in 1813 and settled in Jersey where ten years later Emile was born, son of a respectable shopkeeper. Popular rumour, however, was ready to claim that he had taken advantage of her innocence with his Gallic charm, had used those indiscreet letters she had written believing him to be in love with her, vile seducer that he was, and when she was to marry William Minnoch, was using them to threaten to tell her father.

But Faro was not convinced and never would be.

He had a moment of sheer panic. But this

girl turning to greet him, Lena/Madeleine, clinging to Erland's arm, did not know him. There was no flicker of recognition in that smile.

Faro shocked beyond speech or thought could think of nothing to say; it was his turn to stammer, following them indoors with the nightmare about to unfold, the peace of Red House to be bitterly ended.

What was he to do? Did Erland know her real identity? That was impossible. He suspected that the inhabitants of Red House, if they were aware of it, would disregard such a scandal, perhaps even relish having such a stunner as a suspected murderess in their midst.

As for himself, Lena could not be expected to remember the uniformed and helmeted constable who had been allotted to assist her exit via the back door of the Edinburgh High Court. A young woman from the courtroom's audience who had attended most of the trial was persuaded by Madeleine's defence lawyer to exchange clothes with her and, thus veiled, was hustled out to the waiting carriage to lure the crowds away.

Not that those crowds were hostile. By no means. Far from it. Most were cheering. Madeleine had smiled shyly at them, and their hearts went out to her, so serene and composed in court, so brave. How could this gently brought up, lovely young girl have poisoned her seducer, that Frenchman chap, a common, flash, shallow womaniser.

But Emile L'Angelier was more than a lover. He and Madeleine referred to themselves in their letters as husband and wife. And that in Scots common law, according to Faro, was regarded as 'marriage by habit and repute'.

He remembered as he had emerged with Madeleine Smith from the court's back entrance, she had raised her eyes to him gratefully, eyes the dark blue of innocent summer flowers and Faro knew in that one glance that, even aware that she was guilty, he had sympathy for the jury. With already enough of the detective inborn to recognise, to sift through evidence and come to his own conclusions, whatever his heart might declare as a man, the evidence—remembering her declaration and the letters read in court—said she was guilty.

But as a man he understood the emotions of that male jury, many of them middle-class Edinburgh citizens, some with young unmarried daughters just like her. He had sympathy for them. How would they live with their consciences afterwards—would they lie sleepless at night wondering if they had given the wrong verdict? Only two had called for the guilty verdict and he could imagine how they were shouted down. They could not hang her. Such a verdict would have met with public outrage.

Now walking a few steps behind Erland, who had his arm about his bride-to-be, Faro was faced with a dilemma indeed.

Erland obviously had no idea of her true identity. She had lied to him, presented an ingenuous story about being orphaned, an aunt who had died. She would consider herself safe in the bohemian circle of Red House.

But would she be content to marry Erland and bury the past or was he merely a stepping stone to something greater? She was capable of sexual passion, no one could doubt. This Faro knew from the evidence and those love letters to Emile, so explicit that the court realised they were too indecent to be read out loud.

Suddenly at his side, behind Lena and Erland, he was aware of a pretty girl, her companion who had emerged from the wagonette. He had been introduced to her, but in his all-consuming anxiety, he had promptly forgotten her name.

She was laden with parcels and, remembering his manners, he took them from her, this humble act of chivalry rewarded with a sweet smile as she looked up into his face. Now she was talking, telling him all about their shopping expedition to London, what a splendid visit and how they had been lavishly entertained by such a nice man, a special friend of Topsy, his business manager called George Wardle.

Faro was hardly listening, following Erland into the house, who looked over his shoulder and gave him a knowing wink at the girl on his arm and called, 'Jeremy will take good care of you, Poppy.'

The front door closed behind them and at once Faro bowed, put down the parcels, made his excuses and fled to his room with its Gothic windows and wall slits for arrows, as if this was indeed a medieval castle and he was a condemned man.

Glad to be alone, he groaned.

What on earth was he to do? He could not stand by his friend's side at the altar in a few days' time and ignore the fact that he knew 'just cause and impediment why these two should not be joined together in holy matrimony'.

Now remembering those past schooldays in Orkney how Erland had relied upon him to fight his battles, could he choose that moment to publicly blight his future, break his heart?

One thing was certain. He could not remain in Red House any longer. He must make an excuse, tell a lie, say that Macheath had been spotted and that he must go in pursuit.

But even as he seized his few possessions and thrust them into his valise, he knew he could not do it. Such was the coward's way out. Even if he left, his action could certainly not stop Erland going to the church and taking Lena Hamilton alias Madeleine Smith, the Glasgow poisoner, as his wedded wife.

That was bad enough but what of the future? What of Erland's own safety should some more attractive possibility come her way, another William Minnoch who had a great deal more to offer.

A way out of this dire situation must be found. Who was this George Wardle that Poppy had been so enthusiastic about, and his warm reception during their London shopping visit? He must find out more about him.

As the occupants of the house assembled for the evening meal, at the gong's loud summons Morris came up from the cellar, beaming with joy, his hands full of wine bottles with more tucked rather perilously under his arms while Faro's fears of getting through the evening were relieved by the absence of Erland and Lena, as well as Poppy. The trio, he was told, had been invited to dine with the local minister.

But seated at that round table, a gastronomic delight was in store: a splendid meal of gargantuan proportions. There was a leg of lamb from the local butcher, a variety of vegetables and fruit home-grown in the gardens, and apples and blackberries for a rich dessert.

Each course was accompanied by fine wines. Faro had learnt his lesson and he was cautious, keeping a watchful eye on the bottle being passed around the table and being strong enough to refuse the constant refills.

His companions were less circumspect. Morris was the reincarnation of a medieval host and when he wanted to make a point in his loud conversations, he would spring from his seat at the table into the middle of the room and flourish his fists, ready to fight anyone who disagreed with him. Such actions were greeted by roars of laughter and jeering, teasing comments, while the apples that had not found their way into the dessert but were reclining in a bowl alongside pears and oranges would be pelted at him.

This behaviour caused a great deal of merriment with music hall songs in abundance and, as the wine took effect, Faro found himself caught up in the general innocent horse-play as befitted the medieval atmosphere.

As he went up to bed at last, yawning and well-fed, his senses lulled by good living, he put aside his misgivings regarding Erland and told himself that a way must be found out of this tricky situation, but tomorrow would do for that.

Tonight all he welcomed was sleep and his last thought as he closed his eyes was of Lena's friend Poppy. She had paid him a lot of attention. Every time he glanced her way, she seemed to be smiling at him, her eyes shining.

He sighed. Such a pretty girl.

CHAPTER SIX

Next morning, there was a breakfast as huge as the evening meal consisting mostly of cooked ham, kidneys, tea, jam and what the assembled company referred to as Topsy's 'horrid eggs', a huge platter which he consumed in vast quantities. Faro ate little as, seeing Erland, all his anxieties were renewed. The two lovers were engrossed in themselves, seemingly so happy and carefree that his conscience smote him anew. If only he knew what was right, what to do.

Aware of his inexperience he would have given much for the advice McFie had to offer in plenty. He had never approved of this assignment and Faro, visiting him before he left Edinburgh, had found the retired inspector taken aback at Noble's order to send the young policeman down to Kent in pursuit of a desperate criminal and murderer and alone to bring Macheath back to Scotland to stand trial. Shaking his head sadly he said: 'They certainly do things differently since my day.'

In retrospect Faro felt there was something ominous in the old detective's words. He had sent him the promised letter that he had arrived safely at Upton and was staying at Red House. Now in despair, he thought if only he could explain his predicament to McFie who would probably be in Sussex at this moment on his annual visit to his married sister. Alas, he did not know her address and by the time a letter marked urgent was forwarded from Edinburgh and a reply reached him, Erland and Lena would be married.

Faro realised how much he had come to value McFie's support. Newly arrived in Edinburgh, his fellow constables tormented him with their unceasing teasing. 'This foreigner from Orkney—where on God's earth was that and did they still live in caves?' Their attitude was not much improved when rumour reached them that on the recommendation of Chief Inspector McFie the lowly beat policeman would shortly be promoted to Detective Constable.

McFie had become his ally after Faro saved his life—so McFie claimed—by racing after his runaway carriage, leaping on to the horse's back and bringing it to a standstill as it toppled on the icy slope of the Mound.

His bravery earned him a grudging though scornful respect from his colleagues although Faro had not then known the occupant's identity until he was called into the inner office.

McFie was grateful, wanted to know all about him, his background and his father, Constable Magnus Faro's fatal accident. They had never met as McFie had been serving with the Aberdeen police at that time.

McFie learnt that young Faro was alone; his mother, blaming the Edinburgh police for her husband's death, had returned to Orkney and had never quite forgiven their only son Jeremy for not staying in Kirkwall and making a decent Orcadian living from the fishing and the land as his ancestors had done. Instead he had rushed off to that dangerous, wicked mainland and the city that had killed her man.

Faro found the old inspector, a long-time widower and about to retire, very sympathetic. His only son, who had been killed in a riding accident, would have been Faro's age. Had he been less than a practical, no-nonsense policeman and more of a God-fearing citizen, he might have allowed thoughts that Faro had been sent by divine providence to replace his lost son.

Whatever his secret thoughts, when McFie retired he kept in touch with Jeremy Faro through a weekly meeting at a local inn, then, realising that Faro was in the rather basic lodgings provided for unmarried constables, their meeting was transformed into an evening meal at McFie's home in Nicholson Square prepared by his housekeeper, a young highly efficient woman called Mrs Brook.

So began a friendship between the lonely old man who sadly missed the Edinburgh police and felt that he had been put out to graze far too soon with many years of criminal investigation still in him. Faro became his link with those past days and the present, keeping him in touch with the comings and goings, especially DS Noble, newly arrived from Glasgow and keen on throwing his weight about, especially in young Faro's direction for whom he seemed to have taken an instant and quite irrational antipathy.

McFie knew the type well: older, more experienced officers who felt threatened by clever young constables and enjoyed cutting them down to size. Well, he had certainly achieved this in sending young Faro down to Kent, to single-handedly bring back a wanted man. He would be very lucky indeed to survive. The waste of a good policeman, thought McFie, shaking his head sadly at the news.

*   *   *

Now in Red House, walking the floor of his room, with Erland and Lena's voices reaching him from the garden far below, Faro remembered how it was McFie's influence that got him to the trial of Madeleine Smith, a trial that took not only Edinburgh and Glasgow but the whole of Britain by storm, with daily reports in the national newspapers.

The young woman accused of poisoning her lover with arsenic was from a wealthy, highly respected family of Glasgow architects. Emile

57

L'Angelier, something of a womaniser, was what was commonly known as a waster. Emile had failed to fulfil the early promise of his respectable Jersey family and, on the lookout for a wealthy marriage, had spotted Madeleine and engineered an introduction to her through a common acquaintance.

There was an immediate rapport between the attractive girl and the rather flashy Frenchman some thirteen years her senior, a warehouse clerk with a firm of Glasgow merchants.

Perhaps initially it was the element of danger which appealed to Madeleine, a romantic novelettish relationship that must be kept secret at all cost, breathing an element of excitement and danger into the monotonous upper class-existence of her Glasgow life with its daily ritual of morning prayers and visiting cards for balls and parties.

After their first secret meeting in April 1855, both declared themselves in love and a series of passionate letters—some 400—were exchanged during their relationship and marriage was discussed between them for the following September.

When Madeleine brought up the subject her parents were furious. They refused consent and as she would not be 21 until 1857 there was talk of elopement. However, her parents had other plans and a young man of their own class, William Minnoch, was introduced to the household and became a regular visitor.

Meanwhile the illicit love affair between Emile and Madeleine had reached a climax. They had become lovers but lovers without a hope of marriage. The letters, the secret meetings at night when the family slept or were absent on visits when Madeleine admitted Emile, with the maid's assistance, to the house or if this was impossible to the laundry room, had to stop. It was a situation that could not continue and by January 1857 she had accepted William Minnoch's proposal of marriage, beamed upon and blessed by her parents. But somehow she had to get rid of Emile.

The dream was over, the fun and excitement at an end. Much as she had thought she loved Emile, she knew that marriage was impossible, and exchanging her comfortable upper-class life for a world she did not know, as the wife of a clerk earning £50 per year, was unthinkable.

She proceeded to write a harsh letter at the beginning of February that 'owing to coolness and indifference, we had better for the future consider ourselves as strangers,' adding, 'I trust your honour as a gentleman that you will not reveal anything that may have passed between us,' and asking him to return her letters and likeness that Thursday evening. A dramatic change from the note written only a week before: 'Oh sweet darling, at this moment my heart and soul burn with love for thee, my husband, what would I not give at this moment to be your fond wife.'

There were more hysterical letters as Madeleine begged Emile not to give her away and to destroy the letters. He refused and, as appeals to his chivalry and his sense of fair play were of no avail, Madeleine sent out the Smith family houseboy to purchase a small vial of prussic acid which she said was to clean her hands. The apothecary refused—a few drops could kill a healthy adult.

Meanwhile rumour had reached Emile of her engagement to William Minnoch and he now threatened to reveal all. Those wild indiscreet letters in which she signed herself 'Mimi L'Angelier', as well as bringing down her father's wrath upon her head, would also be an end to any hope of marriage with Minnoch.

Madeleine now knew she had only one way out. To get rid of Emile by any other means available. Arsenic was the next resort.

She said at her trial later that she had read in a magazine, and learnt from a teacher at her boarding school in England, that arsenic was good for the complexion. She did not like to put this as the reason for signing the local apothecary's Poison Book for sixpeny worth of arsenic, so she said that it was to rid the house of rats, a claim vigorously denied by the maid, Christina, who had given Emile, at Madeleine's instruction, late-night access to the house in Blythswood Square. As by law arsenic was coloured blue in case of accidents, the maid had never seen evidence of colour in the blue washbasin she emptied each day after Madeleine's use.

During that February to March, at three secret meetings at Blythswood Square, Madeleine had given Emile a cup of cocoa—it was shown later that this thick liquid would conceal the bitter taste—cocoa, which Christina said Madeleine kept in a packet on the mantelshelf in her room and to which no one else in the family had access.

Madeleine was cautious with the first two attempts, which only made Emile vomit and feel very ill. The third however had the satisfactory conclusion. Emile died.

No longer a threat, only those damning letters remained and Madeleine fled to the family home at Rowaleyn to be brought back by William Minnoch, who must have been utterly bewildered by this turn of events, preparing for his marriage to Madeleine and never having met or heard of his rival.

Two post-mortems on Emile revealed a massive amount of arsenic. He had indeed been poisoned and Madeleine was arrested and charged with his murder.

The result after a trial of nine and a half days, and thirty-five minutes for the jury's verdict, was a Not Proven verdict, which so often was interpreted somewhat cynically as, 'We know you did it but we can't prove you did it, so go away, and don't do it again.'

Faro had kept a log of the trial and the jury's decision in no way curbed the heated debate about the case with possible solutions, both plausible and bizarre, which were to continue to be discussed long afterwards, not least by Faro and McFie.

Both agreed that there were several possible explanations.

The first and most obvious was that if Madeleine had not killed Emile, then he had, in fact, poisoned himself.

'You're implying that he took poison by mistake,' said McFie.

Faro shook his head. 'The problem is that we know from his co-workers and colleagues that he had an aversion to taking medicines of any kind. None at all and certainly no arsenic was found among his possessions after his death.'

'What about suicide then?'

Faro frowned. 'True. But why—the post-mortem revealed a massive dose of arsenic, how then had he obtained it without leaving any record?'

McFie nodded. 'How indeed! There are very strict rules about poisons and his name was not found in the Poison Books in places where he had stayed in Edinburgh, Glasgow or Bridge of Allan—'

'While Madeleine's signature was found in three different apothecaries' books in Glasgow.'

McFie thought for a moment. 'For suicide, in my experience, there had to be a valid reason. In Emile's case, a broken heart at her betrayal would be feasible and a possible desire for revenge.' He shook his head. 'But most suicides leave a note and if he wished to frame Madeleine for his death, then Emile would have to know about those arsenic purchases she made. And there is certainly no evidence of any such knowledge.'

'I agree,' said Faro. 'Then there was that curious matter of his deciding to keep a diary with one line entries, and the initial M or Mimi, for the last two months of his life. Why he did this has never been satisfactorily explained.'

'Nor has that last journey from Bridge of Allan where he had gone to recuperate from what he believed was a fever but was the effects of arsenic poisoning,' said McFie. 'If he intended to kill himself, why did he make that return journey to Glasgow when he was feeling so ill?'

'Let's not forget the significance of those first two bouts of illness. If these were in fact failed attempts at self-destruction, why would he attempt a third time—with arsenic—when the method was so painful and had failed twice? Why not try some other method?'

'Exactly,' said McFie. 'Such as jumping off a railway bridge in the path of an oncoming train, that was always the most popular, or slitting his wrists?'

There was a moment's silence, then McFie said, 'Is there a possibility that someone other than Madeleine murdered Emile purposely or inadvertently implicating Madeleine in his death.'

Faro shook his head. 'Madeleine's defence team never produced any other person who might have wanted him dead, or had a motive for doing so. And while co-workers and colleagues' opinions of Emile varied, even those who did not care for him particularly, calling him shallow, or flashy and vain, that is hardly sufficient reason to want to kill him.'

McFie rubbed his chin thoughtfully. 'You have a point there, Faro—Emile killed by someone and framing Madeleine—well, he or she would have to be in possession of two pieces of vital information, such as being aware that the pair were involved in a romantic and illicit relationship and that Madeleine, wishing to end it, had made recent purchases of arsenic.'

'I've thought a lot about that too,' said Faro. 'Emile's co-workers and Madeleine's maid Christina certainly knew of the love affair. The various Glasgow apothecaries, as well as Madeleine's intended bridesmaid for her wedding to Minnoch—told it was for cosmetic purposes—knew of the arsenic purchases. But the only person who knew of both love affair and the arsenic was Madeleine herself.'

'And if this was a typical love triangle,' McFie put in, 'then Minnoch would be the most likely suspect. But he didn't know of Emile's existence until after his death when Madeleine was arrested which must have been a considerable shock to him.'

Faro was silent for a moment. 'There is one other possibility. What if Emile was killed by a stranger who knew nothing of his relationship with Madeleine Smith? How about that?'

McFie smiled. 'You're in the land of fantasy with this one, lad. For Emile to have come across a murderous stranger or acquaintance on that fatal night and for that person, of all possible murder weapons such as knife, pistol or strangulation, to choose the specific poison that Emile's lover had been purchasing. Well, that theory relies on too many stark coincidences, does it not?'

Faro agreed. 'So we are left with only one conclusion. That Madeleine did in fact kill Emile. But although her purchases of arsenic made a strong case, her lack of an immediate attempt to retrieve those damning letters was on her side. Unless he had been telling her lies about keeping them, which would put an end to any possibility of her marrying Minnoch, then she must have been fully aware of the terrible danger she was in, that they would be found among his possessions.'

'Did she perhaps still have a forlorn hope that her pleas had been successful and that he had destroyed them?'

'Then she had killed him for nothing, you mean. A terrible thought. I can't believe that she was so naive, knowing that her maid could testify about Emile's visits and those cups of cocoa.'

'There is still one mystery unsolved,' Faro said. 'Those five missing hours on March 22 from when he was last seen heading in the direction of Blythswood Square and his death in his lodgings in the early hours of the following morning. He was unable to tell anyone about that "dark liquid" he had recently consumed but colleagues and his old friend Mary Perry remembered that in the weeks before his death he had mentioned the possibility of his being poisoned.

'Whatever the reason for his silence as he lay dying in agony, he must have suspected the cocoa he had recently consumed was responsible. But he died without naming the obvious person, his lover Madeleine, and that remains the greatest puzzle.'

Pausing for a moment, he added: 'Or did he still love her right to the end and, remembering the once close relationship, did he refuse to believe that she was capable of doing him harm? So without any accusation, it was circumstantial evidence only that saved her from the gallows and got that "Not Proven" verdict.'

The older man had smiled wryly. 'Aye, lad,

had that jury been women, then the outcome might have been different.' And laying aside Faro's comprehensive notes, he said, 'We'll make a detective of you yet, Faro.'

CHAPTER SEVEN

Now, three years later, in the impersonal surroundings of Red House, Faro groaned anew. How would his old friend have dealt with this new crisis, this diabolical situation in which he found himself? He heard his name called; something hit his window. There were shouts of laughter as he looked towards the orchards. Erland had emerged with Lena from the summerhouse, a romantic setting secluded from the rest of the garden.

Erland, ready to throw another apple, grinned up at him. 'Don't be shy, Jeremy, come and join us. Lena is dying to talk to you.'

Faro went slowly down the stairs. He couldn't avoid Lena for ever. Meeting her in Red House was inevitable. As for that approaching wedding—he had to think of something but his wits had temporarily deserted him.

Stepping out into the sunshine, he braced himself for this second encounter. In normal circumstances he would have been overcome with joy. For this was indeed a new Erland he

67

beheld, transformed by the presence of the girl he knew and loved as Lena. No longer weak and indecisive, the pale crippled schoolboy who had suffered from fainting fits had become a strong handsome and virile young man, radiant in countenance and confident in the future.

How could Jeremy Faro, the friend whom he believed was more than that—kin who could be trusted—now with his terrible knowledge, use the power in his hands to ruin for ever that image of hope and happiness.

As he reached them in the little courtyard, he saw the two lovers were absorbed in each other, Lena snuggling into Erland's side, smiling up into his face. She looked so young, so pretty and wistful and—dear God, so innocent—Faro found himself remembering that was exactly how she had appeared during her trial.

Hardly hearing their bright conversation about those inevitable wedding arrangements, he saw instead that hot dusty Edinburgh courtroom waiting for the trial to begin, the room packed, the audience noisy with clerks hurrying among the desks, distributing papers and official documents. A sudden hush as judges and lawyers took their seats, an absolute silence of anticipation as a trapdoor in the floor opened and Madeleine ascended, wearing a brown silk gown, lavender gloves and a white bonnet with a veil.

An artist seated directly below Faro was already busily sketching, possibly for the various newspapers whose reporters were waiting anxiously for her image. Madeleine, as if aware of the artist, turned round to look at the reporters to see how they were getting along with the note taking carrying her name and notoriety into every British home. Not only in Edinburgh and Glasgow newspapers but even the London *Times* carried a daily report of the proceedings.

The prisoner, a young lady of remarkably prepossessing appearance, took her place at the bar with a firm step and a composed aspect, her self-control never forsaking her for a moment . . . she entered the dock with all the buoyancy with which she might have entered the box of a theatre . . . her restless sparkling eyes, her perfect self-possession indeed could only be accounted for either by a proud conscience of innocence, or by her possessing an almost unparalleled amount of self-control. Through her veil she seemed to scan the witnesses with a scrutinising glance and even smiled with all the air and grace of a young lady in the drawing room, as her agents came forward at intervals to communicate with her.

Any man would have considered her desirable. Faro recognised that. Small, slender, vulnerable and quite lovely. She carried a small vial of smelling salts which he never saw her use during that nine-day trial. Her Declaration was read out and verified and the Sheriff remarked that her answers were given clearly and distinctly. There was no appearance of hesitation or reserve but there was a great appearance of frankness and candour.

The audience held their breath as the indictments to murder on three occasions, two in February and one in March, were read aloud.

All eyes turned to Madeleine, who stood up and said in a clear voice, 'Not guilty.' She sat down again, her polite and gentle smile with no more emotion than she would have declined an invitation to a supper party. After that, silence. This was her one and only public utterance for she was not permitted by the law to speak in her own defence.

Faro observed her closely and saw how with every witness her demeanour was the same. Calm and unruffled, she listened with complete attention, sometimes leaning forward and resting her chin on her hand.

Only once, with the recitation of her letters which took an entire day, was there any change in her self-control. But even the flat monotone, the strong Glasgow intonation of the elderly Clerk of the Court, could not disguise the passion and the implications of the word 'love', often underlined emphatically, which indicated that there was indeed a sexual relationship. Some portions, however, were considered too obscene to be read out in court and were excluded by the three judges, and at such announcements she occasionally hid her face in her hands.

*   *   *

As Lena did at that moment. But merely to burst out laughing at something outrageous Erland had whispered and the past of an Edinburgh courtroom momentarily blended into the present—a garden's mellow sunshine, still warm for the winds of autumn had not yet stripped the trees.

Above their heads a robin sang, his sweet serenade adding to that feeling of peace and serenity, of time eternal. Red House, so newly built as a marriage home for William and Janey Morris and a family life still to come, had a sense of belonging to the landscape as if it had been here awaiting their arrival.

Faro bowed rather stiffly over Lena's hand and, smiling, she made room for him on the rustic garden seat. It seemed impossible that she could not recognise him again, although there had been no smiles during their first encounter on that journey from the High Court to Slateford, meeting with her brother James, who would take her back to Glasgow and a reception from her stern father that beggared imagination.

Faro remembered her perfume, a delicate scent of some unknown flowers. The same

71

perfume she still wore and again it touched his senses, his masculinity yearning for this strongly desirable woman. Her slender shape, her features delicate and sharply defined, she would be the perfect model for Rossetti, with a beauty of bone structure that would wear well with time and defy age.

Indeed she looked even younger than she had during the trial, just a mere slip of a girl. Impossible to imagine that the girl before him could have been capable of murdering anyone and against his will he felt a tinge of envy for Emile who had been her lover in the past and for Erland who had this new role in her life.

Erland. He was hardly listening to the radiant Erland saying, 'This is a perfect day for me—' and taking Lena's hand he placed it in Jeremy's, linking the two together. 'You are to be the greatest friends—my wife and my cousin, who is also my dearest friend. If I was a God-fearing man, I would thank the good Lord for this extraordinary coincidence of bringing us together in Red House.' He grinned. 'In God's absence, however, I shall have to thank Topsy Morris.'

Lena listened, smiling, and gently withdrew her hand. 'It is good to meet you, Jeremy. And I share dear Erland's sentiments.'

Did she recognise him? He thought it highly unlikely that she had been aware of his presence among the many onlookers at her trial. Apart from a polite inclination of her

72

head, a thanks for his escort to Slateford, he had not heard her voice until now. A pleasant educated upper-class voice with only the faintest trace of a Scots accent.

'Erland has told me of the marvellous coincidence of you being down here on business.'

Faro gave his friend a sharp glance as Lena said hastily, 'Be assured that I shall be most discreet.'

Erland shifted uncomfortably under his gaze. What kind of business had he invented? Were there any secret hints that he was a policeman?

Lena was smiling, nodding towards the house. 'Not a word to anyone, I promise. I hope you'll complete your assignment but not too soon.' Another tender smile at Erland this time. 'Not until after our wedding or dearest Erland will be so disappointed. And so indeed will I, having met you.'

Quite a fulsome little speech, Faro decided, unable to think of a suitable response, burdened by his own terrible thoughts about the situation he had encountered which seemed more fraught with horror than any possible meeting with his hidden enemy Macheath.

'We are all north Britons,' said Erland, 'although people do confuse Orkney with Scotland, don't they, Jeremy?'

Faro looked at her. A sudden devil in him

made him ask: 'Do you know Edinburgh, Miss Hamilton?'

'Lena, please.' And looking up at the house as if the question required thought, she nodded vaguely. 'Not really at all. I believe my parents took me there when I was a little girl but I have no memory of anything but the magnificent castle. Like something out of a fairy tale.'

'Lena is from Glasgow, Jeremy. There's always been rivalry between the two great cities, as you well know.' Erland sounded apologetic and Lena sighed and nodded.

'I would like to visit Edinburgh some day.'

That was another lie. And watching Erland kiss her hand and whisper, 'And I shall take you there, my darling, perhaps on our honeymoon,' Faro's lips narrowed. He had a sudden irresistible desire to say, 'When you do, you should make a point of visiting the High Court, an unforgettable experience—it is where all the murder trials take place.'

A girl ran out of the house towards them.

'Where have you been, Poppy?" asked Lena jumping to her feet.

'Well might you ask. I thought I'd never get away from him. I'm exhausted, he's been at me all morning,' she groaned.

What on earth was she talking about? Soon it became evident that Lena's friend was another of Rossetti's models.

'Good morning, Jeremy,' she said and held

74

out her hand. As the conversation had turned to exciting feminine matters such as what she had bought in London to wear for the wedding, to which the men were outsiders, Poppy turned to Faro with a comical shrug.

'I hope you are enjoying your visit and that these two aren't boring you to death with their wedding plans.' Pausing to smile indulgently at them, she said, 'It is all their conversation, you would think no one in the world had ever got married since Adam and Eve. Perhaps Jeremy would like me to show him the garden. Come along.'

And as she took his arm in the manner of one who was an old friend—and a very attractive one, Faro had to admit—he decided that the two girls were not unalike in appearance, slender with slight frame and delicate colouring of the type that the artists seemed to admire in their models.

As Poppy steered him towards the summerhouse in its romantic seclusion beyond the rose garden, she did not appear to notice his monosyllabic response to her polite questions, preoccupied as he was with the possibility that Erland had told Lena that he was a policeman and she would remember him as the Edinburgh constable who escorted her from the High Court.

But it was the transformation in Erland that troubled him most. How on earth was he to avert the imminent disaster, the death blow to his happiness when the truth about Lena Hamilton was revealed?

There was an alternative, of course; the only one. To keep that information to himself and leave Erland and Madeleine to their fate.

Fate, however, had other plans and was to take the matter out of Faro's hands in the form of the pre-wedding masque and the advent of a newcomer to Red House, Topsy Morris's business manager, the wealthy and highly eligible bachelor, George Wardle.

CHAPTER EIGHT

There was no escape from the present or the charming girl whose attentions he would have normally found extremely flattering. Leading the way beyond the rose garden to the secluded summerhouse, she indicated one of its rustic seats and asked gently, 'Are you here for your cousin's wedding?'

Faro thought for a moment. A lie perhaps? 'Not entirely. I happened to be in the district on business.'

Had Lena kept Erland's promise of secrecy or did she also know that he was a policeman?

Poppy looked at him eagerly, her expression demanding further information and he said, 'I'm here on business for an Edinburgh client.'

'You are in property then?'

'In a way.' That much was vaguely true.

'When did you last see Erland?'

'A long time ago. In Orkney when we were young, at school in fact . . .'

She frowned. 'How odd—I thought you were in constant touch with one another—being cousins, family and that sort of thing—'

She sounded reproachful and he hastily interrupted. 'He isn't really my cousin.'

'But he said—'

'His family and mine are distantly related—in a small island community that often happens. We are just school friends from way back although Erland likes to pretend that we are cousins.'

She smiled sadly. 'That is not unreasonable—to claim kinship, when one is alone in the world. I feel so sorry for Lena, you know. A wedding without any family members present.'

A useful introduction to that painful topic, Faro thought, and asked, 'How did you two come to meet?'

'Here. I'm a local lass, got a job as a kitchen maid when Mr Morris was engaging staff for the house. Then on one of his visits Gabriel spotted me and insisted that I should model for him. I was flattered and impressed and, as I'm fond of fine sewing, it sounded like a better option than scrubbing the stairs.'

Faro looked at her unable to believe she had ever served in such a lowly capacity as she went on. 'My mother lives in the village—a widow—I'm the eldest and I have three young sisters—'

'Do you know the miller and his family?' Faro interrupted eagerly. 'I have to visit him.'

Poppy grimaced. 'I don't envy you. From all accounts he is not a nice man, a bully. He has a very bad reputation. Everyone feels sorry for his wife and daughter.'

And that, Faro decided, was the lead he was looking for as he asked, 'Is Bess a friend of yours?'

She shook her head. 'Hardly know her. She's a bit younger than me.' A shrug. 'Quite frankly, Mam didn't like us associating with the Tracys.' Her reticence explained many things to Faro without the need to ask any more questions. There was one Poppy put to him.

'Why do you ask?' And a curious glance. 'What's your interest in Bess?'

'Oh, just part of my enquiries.'

Poppy gave a wry smile. 'I gather Bess always has plenty to say to a good-looking man. She won't fail you there, for sure.'

She laughed and her knowing glance made him uncomfortable. He would have liked to ask if she knew Bess was missing, but such a question would require a tortuous explanation that he was not at all keen to give.

Changing the subject he said quickly, 'You get along very well with Lena.'

She nodded. 'I do indeed. She is my best friend. From the moment she arrived with Erland. I would do anything for her. She is a wonderful person, so kind and understanding with everyone.'

They were no longer alone in the garden. A lot of unseen activity nearby indicated the gardeners were approaching.

A group of hooded figures came into view. Sacking over their heads and shoulders, protection from the weather and doubtless the falling apples they gathered, transformed them into medieval figures from an ancient pastoral tapestry, a picture of harmony in keeping with their surroundings as they toured the gardens with their wheelbarrows.

Two of the group were engaged nearby in the thornier prospect of trimming the roses chatting amiably to each other but this was hardly a suitable moment for Faro to dash off, leaving Poppy without explanation, to elicit possible information about Bess's swain.

As he watched them with suppressed frustration, wondering if one of the two fitted the role of Bess's 'very respectable chap', perhaps imagining that his preoccupation was boredom, Poppy asked, 'Do you like roses? Topsy would only allow those of the perfumed variety, he said roses had to smell like roses or they were just a hollow mockery. On his instruction the petals are all harvested and made into perfume by the ladies. Look, here he is.'

Poppy waved to Morris and he approached with his easel from the direction of the shrubbery where he had been making sketches of various wild flowers, destined to play their part in designs for one of his wallpaper and tapestry projects.

Faro observed that there was considerably more paint on his clothes and hair than was justified by painting a few flowers and, in fact, he looked more of a labouring man than the gardeners, whose garb was neat and tidy by comparison.

Poppy greeted him with a polite good day but, almost embarrassed by this encounter, Morris merely stared at her and at Faro as if he had never seen either of them before. With a bow, a puzzled frown and mumbled response, head down, he darted towards the courtyard.

Faro decided that he was not the only one who suffered from preoccupation as Poppy whispered, 'He's like that. Totally absorbed in whatever he is doing at the moment—'

The sound of a gong nearby erupted into the silence, frightening birds enjoying a quiet siesta on their various tree perches, into noisy squawking flight.

'What on earth is that?' Faro demanded.

Poppy leapt to her feet. 'That's for me. I must go.'

'Have they no clocks in the house?'

Poppy smiled. 'Gabriel needs me again. The gardens are so large, we are all apt to get lost. He is sure we will wander away and this is his way to summon back to the studio his models out for a breath of air. I enjoy sitting for him, it's easy work and I earn a lot more than I did in the kitchens,' she added candidly, her sigh and wistful glance indicating that she would have much preferred to stay with her new companion.

A house without clocks, a medieval garden with gardeners to match. He felt as if he had stepped back in time. Only the chug-chug of an engine, a puff of smoke from the nearby railway line as a train headed towards London reassured him that this was indeed the year 1860.

Now that Mr Morris had departed, the hooded figures were taking an early break from their labours, talking and laughing together as they did justice to pies and mugs of ale brought over by two of the kitchen maids, who received plenty of flirtatious comments in recompense. One of the men might well be the missing Bess's suitor, Faro decided. But as he walked purposefully towards them, they all looked round, sprang to their feet and stared at him, not in an unfriendly manner but just polite and curious.

'Is there something the matter, sir?' one asked.

How could he respond? It was impossible to

ask that question, it sounded too banal—and embarrassing. Yet the question must be asked.

'I was looking for a young lady. Bess Tracy—do any of you know her?'

Knowing looks were exchanged, a nudge, a giggle suppressed. Obviously Muir was right about Bess Tracy's reputation, reinforced by Poppy's hints. And those arch glances from the gardeners, surveying this well-dressed man, this toff, shouted his intentions louder than any words, that rumours had reached him regarding the remarkable abilities of the local whore.

As heads were shaken, Faro realised that he lacked the courage to turn his back and walk swiftly away. Instead he lingered, expressing a sudden interest in the variety of apples, enquiring which of them were mostly used for cooking.

This brought an unexpected bout of enthusiasm and it was with some difficulty that he managed to extract himself from the merits of the varieties whose names he would never remember.

Making his escape at last, he took out his pocket watch. Time for his dismal routine visit to the police office. How long would this continue, the daily telegraph to Noble that no progress had been made. The same wording: 'No sighting to report. Await your further instructions.' And an hour later the inevitable response. 'Continue your search. Remain vigilant.'

The whole situation was ludicrous. For one thing, although he had seen Macheath's face at close quarters as they fought on that lonely stretch of beach at Portabello, his quarry— who was of medium height, strong and athletically built in his late thirties or early forties—had a dark beard which concealed any distinctive features. And a beard was an excellent disguise. Facial hair was the current fashion and all that was required was for him to shave it off and dye his hair for a new, relatively unrecognisable personality to emerge.

But Faro failed in all his attempts to tactfully convince DS Noble of this rather obvious fact and that this was a waste of police time and their expenses.

Noble had merely laughed, and smiled—a rare thing indeed, leaving Faro to ignore the sarcasm in his smooth response: 'Ah yes, indeed, Constable, so it seems. But if anyone can find Macheath, you are the man for the job. The Edinburgh folk obviously have great faith in you.'

Constable Muir certainly did not share Noble's sentiments. He made no secret of his opinion that the man must be mad. However, he was consoled by saying it could be worse and that Faro had at least found himself a cushy billet for his futile investigation.

'Any further news about the missing girl?'

Muir shook his head. 'Not a whisper.'

Faro regarded him sternly. 'Don't you think it's about time for an investigation?'

Muir laughed. 'Investigation, Faro. Never! Only if her family asked us and they aren't apparently worried.'

'Her mother seemed to be.'

'Aye, poor soul. But with a man like she's got, she's prone to fear the worst.' Leaning back in his chair, he puffed away at the fierce-smelling pipe. 'Besides, when you talk of investigation, you're forgetting something. This isn't a big city like Edinburgh with a whole police force to call on. There's just me on my lonesome and how would I begin to look for a missing girl, who probably just left home in a huff after another row with her father?' He shrugged. 'Happens all the time. Lord above, I'd be doing it every day of the week, Sundays included—'

'I am most willing to give you a hand,' Faro interrupted. Such a task would be infinitely preferable to sitting in Red House and trying to decide whether or not to tell Erland that his Lena had possibly poisoned her last lover.

Muir was eyeing him mockingly. 'Experienced in this sort of thing, are you then? Bit off your patch, ain't it?' He laughed. 'But looking for missing girls is a nice change for a beat policeman. Right up your street.'

And that in all truth was exactly PC Faro's role. Despite McFie's faith in him, he had yet to prove himself—by finding that needle in a haystack, Macheath.

CHAPTER NINE

Before returning to the house, Faro decided to call upon Mrs Lunn at Brettle Manor, regarding the expected return date of the owners in order to legally tie up any loose ends. An excuse, of course, for a further inspection of the kitchen where he suspected Macheath, rather than a passing vagrant, had broken a window and stolen food from the pantry.

As he entered the grounds, distant chimney smoke from the ruinous cottage indicated habitation and skirting some trees he observed the ancient Jim Boone sitting by his front door, clay pipe in hand, an old felt hat pulled down well over his eyes, giving the impression that the passing of time was no longer one of his immediate concerns.

Remembering his friendly greeting in the village street, Faro decided that further conversation with a long-time resident might be well worthwhile. Advancing briskly towards the cottage he called, 'Good day'. Unable to see the expression on the man's bewhiskered face, his threatening gesture however could not be mistaken for a welcome:

'Keep yer distance. This is private property. Come any nearer and I'll set me dog on ye.' With those words he retreated indoors and banged the door shut.

Faro was a little taken aback by this reception. Charitably he decided that Boone's eyesight was poor with age or, according to his reputation as an eccentric, he was in one of his famous bad moods. With a shrug, he proceeded to the house but Mrs Lunn was either not at home or not receiving callers. Fortunately she did not have a dog. He fancied she might well resort to the same lengths as the old fellow in the cottage.

Frustrated by this waste of time, he would have liked to know the reason why she had pretended to discover the broken window when it was Bess Tracy who had done so and notified Constable Muir. This question raised several possibilities, the most interesting being that Mrs Lunn had her own reasons for perhaps wishing to conceal the break-in.

Standing back from the house, he noticed it had a deserted air. As he walked around the outside, whatever he was hoping to find, there was no evidence in the garden. He did notice a succession of neatly trimmed, tall hedges which would in time totally conceal Boone's offending cottage.

His thoughts turned again to those gardeners at Red House. Did all large houses employ their own outdoor staff or did any of those he had seen at Red House also work at Brettle Manor? If so, he would have liked a word with the one Mrs Tracy had told him was keeping company with Bess.

It was now late afternoon, the mellow sunshine casting a deep golden glow over the landscape and, again hearing the distant vibration of a railway engine and a plume of smoke heading northwards, he wished he was a passenger on that train destined for Edinburgh. The fine adventure, the enforced holiday, had lost all taste for him since the revelations concerning Erland and his bride-to-be.

If only Erland had not spotted him on his arrival in Upton. A few moments later and there would have been no accidental meeting and Faro would never have known what became of Madeleine Smith after she left Scotland, or the nightmare situation his knowledge of her identity—and the lies she had told Erland—placed him in.

His spirit shrank from destroying Erland but was all really lost? Could he take a chance on a reformed Madeleine who had reinvented herself and was prepared for a happy future, forgetting all that was past, as Erland Flett's wife, 'until death do us part'?

He hoped so but the shadow of Emile L'Angelier refused to be banished. She had killed one lover and, given the right circumstances, the hand of fate in dealing a new card, he suspected she might just as readily destroy another.

* * *

Erland caught up with him as he reached the house, an excited, exhilarated Erland who had been to the local parish church about 'matters regarding the wedding. Lena and the ladies, Georgie and Janey, will be decorating the church with flower garlands.'

He gave Faro an impish sideways glance. 'How did you enjoy being among the roses with Miss Poppy?'

'A charming girl,' said Faro.

Erland rubbed his hands delightedly. 'That is good—very good indeed. A man in love can easily recognise the symptoms in his best friends. And I gather Miss Poppy is very taken with a certain gentleman from Scotland.'

'Who told you that?' Faro demanded sharply.

Erland laughed. 'As if you didn't know. Girls who are best friends also exchange confidences. It appears that one of her grandparents, Lena tells me, is from Edinburgh and she has always wanted to return, to track down her roots.'

She had omitted this information from their conversation, but it would probably come out at their next meeting as Erland paused, obviously expecting a response. 'How about you, Jeremy?'

'What do you mean—how about me?'

Erland shuffled uncomfortably. 'Don't be difficult—you know what I'm getting at.' And taking a deep breath, 'I mean, do you fancy her? She is an absolute stunner. Nearly as lovely as my Lena.'

Another pause and Faro, determined not to be helpful, murmured, 'So?'

'Listen to me, Jeremy, I'm saying this in all sincerity and for your own good. You don't have to marry this young woman in Edinburgh, do you? What I mean is, things haven't progressed to the stage where you feel obliged—well, to do the honourable thing by her?'

Faro stopped in his tracks and stared at Erland, who went on hastily, 'What I'm trying to say is she is only someone you are keeping company with and there is nothing binding in that, should you meet someone else, that is.'

Faro seized his arm. 'Erland—hold on! I've just met Poppy. She seems a nice enough girl, but I'm not the type to fall in love at first sight—'

'Like me,' whispered Erland.

'Like you then. I need to get to know someone, spend some time with them, find out what we have in common, what we both like and so forth before I commit myself.'

In truth he felt guilty now for he had thought little about Lizzie since his arrival in Upton. They did not have any arrangement for regular meetings, in the way of courting couples. He had not even written to her, telling himself that he would be back in Edinburgh in a day or two.

'But, Jeremy, dear fellow,' Erland was saying. 'Time isn't on your side with Poppy. This is a perfect opportunity. You might have to go back to Scotland any day now and then you'll never meet her or anyone like her ever again. But if you think you could fall in love, given time, that she might be the right one for you, then you could get married with us—a double wedding—'

Pausing, he beamed at Faro and continued excitedly, 'I'm sure that could be arranged; the vicar is a nice man, so understanding. And it would make us both so happy, Lena and me. She would be your cousin-in-law and we would be friends for always. Think of that.'

The idea of being related to Madeleine Smith, murderess, made Faro shudder but he managed a laugh. 'Not a chance, Erland. How you do race along. I need more than a pretty face and an hour's acquaintance—'

'You refuse to be convinced that I'm right.' Erland frowned.

'I do.'

'Let's hope you never regret it—'

Mercifully their conversation was cut short as the door behind them opened and Lena appeared.

'I've been looking for you everywhere,

dearest.' And as if noticing Faro for the first time, 'Will you excuse us, Jeremy?' And with a smile, 'Could you do me the greatest favour?' A shiver and she added, 'I left my shawl in Gabriel's studio. Do you think you could get it for me? I need to talk urgently to Erland.'

Faro could hardly refuse. His wanderings on the upper floor, looked down upon by murals of King Arthur and his Knights and their ladies, made him decide he must find out more, read Tennyson's *Morte d'Artur* since his only acquaintance with Britain's legendary ruler was from Edinburgh's Arthur's Seat. The Gaelic 'Ard na said' claimed to be one of his many resting places. According to the local story, the King and his Knights slept within a secret cave deep inside the mountain, seated at a round table, horns at the ready, deerhounds at their feet, all awaiting the call, ready to ride out and fight Britain's foes, as yet unspecified.

A pretty romantic legend, but not one in which the practical Jeremy Faro could place any belief.

Unsure of where to find Rossetti's studio, he found his way by accident into that occupied by Morris, whose curly head was down low over the drawing board, deep in concentration, the floor strewn with crumpled papers, obviously rejections. As Faro entered, another landed at his feet, followed by an angry expletive.

Faro coughed apologetically. Without looking up, Morris gestured with his paintbrush towards a chair.

'Hand me that, will you.'

'That' was a lump of stale bread that occupied the seat. Faro did as he was bid. Snatching it from him, Morris said, 'Best possible thing for erasing. Try it, you'll see.'

Faro apologised for interrupting, explained that he was looking for Gabriel's studio and was told it was down the corridor, on the left.

He found the door slightly open. On a raised dais, a girl lay on a couch, her naked back towards the artist. A beautiful body indeed, with long slender legs. As he entered, she lifted her head and winked at him.

The nude was Poppy, and Faro found his heart pounding.

Rossetti seemed unaware of his presence, frowning, concentrating on his painting.

Faro stammered an excuse. Lena's shawl.

Rossetti barely glanced around. 'Well, did you see her leave it, Poppy? Don't move, for heaven's sake, keep that pose,' he added anxiously.

Poppy squinted up at Faro. 'She didn't leave it here, but she can have mine. It's over there. I have a jacket—'

Gabriel looked round wildly, paintbrush in hand and pointed.

Faro had to go behind the easel and the artist smiled at him. 'I'm making this pretty lady into one of Rome's tragic heroines. A new departure from Morte d'Artur.'

Faro looked at the canvas. There wasn't much to see yet in those preliminary splashes of paint, which would in due course hang in a London gallery, immortalised as one of Rossetti's great masterpieces.

'Lucrece was raped by wicked Sextus Tarquinius. I'll be summoning up the rest of the cast, once I get her finished.' Pausing, he regarded Faro thoughtfully. 'How do you fancy the role of the wicked rapist,' and narrowing his eyes, 'I can see you—perfectly splendid in a suit of gleaming armour I'm sure Topsy will provide. What do you say? Just a few sittings, that's all.'

Muttering that he would think about it, his face now scarlet at Gabriel's suggestion of his role in the painting, Faro seized Poppy's shawl and fled.

He was halfway downstairs when embarrassment turned to anger. Opening the front door, he heard sounds of laughter from Erland and Lena seated in the courtyard and it took little imagination to be certain that Lena had never left her shawl in Rossetti's studio.

She—and doubtless Erland too—had arranged this little episode so that he should see Poppy at her most seductive.

CHAPTER TEN

Lena accepted the shawl without any trace of embarrassment. Why should she, thought Faro, who after all had considerable experience in concealing guilt over a murdered man, express any emotion over a mere lie regarding a shawl.

As she edged closer along the seat to make room for him, Erland said, 'Lena has had a great idea. George Wardle is here on business to see Topsy and she thought it would be nice on such a lovely day, as an introduction to the area, to take him on a picnic. There's a lovely spot near the mill stream. Just perfect, pretty as any of Ned Burne-Jones's pastoral paintings.'

Pausing with an affectionate look at Lena, he leant over, kissed her cheek and said, 'I have to tell you that this darling girl has been very busy preparing things. I might add that she's perfect in the kitchen, getting in a little practice to be the perfect wife.'

Lena gave him a shy smile, pointing to the picnic hamper alongside. 'Hardly—all I have done is to make a stack of sandwiches for three hungry men.'

Faro eyed her doubtfully. Lena and food did not go well together in his estimation. 'And something to drink, too,' Erland laughed.

Faro bit back the words, 'Not cocoa, I trust,' as Erland added, 'Wine—lots of Topsy's wine, perfect for an autumn day.'

They heard voices from inside the house as Poppy appeared, now fully clothed, followed by George Wardle. A discussion about jackets and umbrellas, which would not be needed, and suitable shoes, then they were ready to depart.

The only one who seemed too well dressed and formal for such an excursion was Wardle, Faro thought. All he lacked was a top hat, which he no doubt had left inside the house. Frock-coated, with a bright waistcoat and tapered trousers, elegant highly polished boots, he presented the perfect picture of the affluent London businessman. A strong face, a fine beard and moustache, he was imposing, a little staid and quietly attractive, rather than handsome. In his favour, although in his late thirties and still unmarried, he was the perfect catch for any designing woman.

Poppy seemed to think so. Slightly disappointed, Faro saw the two girls link arms with Wardle while he and Erland were left to carry the picnic basket between them.

As they walked the short distance to the mill stream their path led past the Mill Cottage looking oddly deserted. No sounds of sawing, no evidence of the distraught Mrs Tracy. Guiltily, Faro's thoughts flew to the missing girl and the policeman in him said that he ought to be investigating that case instead of making merry with these four companions, the girls singing happily as they walked.

And yet there was reason for happiness. There is something about a sunny autumn day that is irresistible, as if summer, determined not to be banished for another year, has made one more dramatic farewell performance. The countryside around them gleamed, the fields heavy with corn ripe for harvest, the tall treetops already tinged with the red and gold that would transform this small piece of Kent with its undulating hills into a paint box of glowing colour.

Faro sighed. Narrowing his eyes, he tried to think ahead, to see it as it would be and for a moment he wished he had the ability to shift time forward, glimpse into that glorious autumn. For in a week or so, and certainly before these trees were winter-bare, he would be back on his beat, Edinburgh's Leith Walk.

By then Erland's wedding would be over— whether it took place or not. And for good or ill, no longer his responsibility.

He thrust aside melancholy thoughts of the immediate future. Today was one to remember and he would not sully this delightful interlude with fears for a future that lay in destiny's hands. Today he would relish this small fragment of near paradise, let it take its place stored away with other past memories, the experience of Red House and the acquaintance of three remarkable men, Morris, Rossetti and Burne-Jones.

As the picnic spot was selected and mutually agreed upon, the bank of a stream shaded by willows, a tablecloth laid on the grass, the contents of the hamper spread out, sandwiches opened by the two girls, the wine uncorked, the glasses filled, Faro wondered how Wardle would react to this cheery informality.

Observing him a little closer as he was drawn into the general conversation, it was soon clear that Wardle could hold his own in any society. Cultured and knowledgeable he slipped into the chat that he had been educated at a 'good', i.e. public, school.

It was also soon clear to Faro, if not to the other members of their party, that Wardle was very obviously smitten with Lena. Was it his imagination, Faro decided, or did he direct all his looks and answers to questions towards her in particular? If he did so, then Erland did not—or pretended not to—notice, beyond regarding any man as his rival so certain was he of Lena's love, with marriage only a couple of days away.

Poppy, it seemed, was also a keen observer and as soon as they reached the picnic site she tactfully abandoned Wardle and devoted all her attention to Faro, who was pleased and, he had to admit, a little flattered. However, seeing her in the pretty muslin dress with covering jacket, he could not quite clear his mind of that earlier picture of the naked girl on Gabriel's studio couch.

He had never seen a completely naked woman before—except in French postcards circulated around the police station in Edinburgh. Brought up in an Orkney of capricious weather where folk of necessity kept well clad, not many clothes were removed even to go to bed at night and he supposed all lovemaking and conception was carried out under the bedclothes.

Seeing Poppy in the flesh, so to speak, had been a strange and exciting experience. He had never made love to Lizzie, and he had told Erland the truth that nothing had progressed between them further than a few chaste kisses. He had not until now thought of what it would be like to be married to Lizzie or any woman, for he could no longer be unaware, as Erland had hinted, that Poppy fancied him.

Although imagination failed to provide any future with this pretty girl and Erland's fantastic idea of a double wedding was too ridiculous to take seriously, he still felt that he had some slight obligation to his past two years of what most folk would describe as 'courting' Lizzie.

Perhaps he was taking it all too seriously and Poppy's role was merely to be the memory of a what-might-have-been, a romantic interlude in Kent.

At his side she stifled a yawn. Wardle's rather

pompous talk of his achievements in the London business world and his talk of William Morris were becoming a little tedious. Here was a man who certainly enjoyed holding centre stage.

Poppy, as though aware of Faro's lack of interest, touched his arm and nodded towards the grassy slope behind them, a copse of trees crowning its summit.

'There's a splendid view over the whole county from there,' she whispered. 'Shall we?'

Without making any excuse that would appear obvious, they left the group, their exit causing no comment apart from a sharp look from Lena and another of Erland's knowing winks.

Taking Faro's arm, Poppy led the way up the little hill, where the tall trees fluttered a welcome as they leant on a fence. Below them, interspersed by the tiny shapes of farms and churches, a patchwork of quilt-like fields stretched out and folded their way in shades of green and gold to disappear in the muted blue of a far horizon.

'Lovely, isn't it? Was it worth the climb?' Poppy asked with a teasing smile.

Faro laughed. 'Indeed,' and added, 'A worthy escape.'

Poppy chuckled. 'I see what you mean. He can be a little boring, poor George. But he is so good and kind, he means well and—' Her voice dropped to an awed whisper as if they might be overheard. 'He simply dotes on Lena, poor man. Doesn't seem to care that there's absolutely no hope for him, that she's to be married to Erland in a day or two. Do you know, he asked her to marry him when we were in London together? Please don't tell Erland...'

'As if I would. Do you think he might challenge him to a duel or something?'

'Of course not. He has no reason to be jealous—not at this late stage.'

But Wardle's infatuation did seem extraordinary. Here was this rich man, a very eligible bachelor, with much of London's society at his door, according to the tale he was still spinning to Erland and Lena down the hill there, ready to ask a woman to marry him on a few hours' acquaintance. This was an emotion that Faro had never known and probably never would.

To fall in love at first sight. Yet Erland claimed to have done so too. He looked at Poppy. Was he missing something? Tentatively he took her hand and, leaning forward, kissed her gently.

At first nothing happened. The next moment, her eyes filled with tears and, with a hoarse little sob, she whispered, 'Jeremy!'

Throwing her arms around his neck, in a mouth-clinging moist kiss, she thrust her body close. Taken by surprise by this uprush of passion, whatever thoughts and arguments

100

existed in his mind only, his body had its own response.

Looking round he realised they were at a disadvantage, clearly visible to the others down the hill. Poppy was also aware of the fact, and she looked longingly towards the trees. He had little doubt of what was to come next, prepared to follow her. Fate, however, in the shape of George Wardle, had destined otherwise.

A shrill whistle. Erland waving, beckoning urgently.

'What does he want now?' demanded Poppy crossly. 'I don't want to go back yet—do you?' she whispered urgently, clinging to his arm.

Of course he didn't but there was little option as Erland was striding up the grassy slope.

'Come on, you two. Didn't you hear me? We have to go back, I'm afraid.'

'Must we?' said Poppy shortly. 'It's still very early. We've only been here an hour.'

'I know, my dear girl. And it's a shame to have to end it all so soon. But George has just informed us that he has an appointment with Topsy at four. Damned nuisance, but it would look terribly rude if we just sent him on his way.'

Faro wouldn't have cared at that moment. He would not have worried about being rude to George one bit, in fact he would have enjoyed the experience. However, discretion must play a part and an exposed hillside was hardly the right sort of place for the lovemaking he guessed was occupying Poppy's thoughts.

She was holding his hand tightly. He looked at her, shook his head, mouthed, 'Later.' Together they ran back down the hill, where Lena was gathering up the contents of the picnic hamper, helped by George.

As they made their way back to Red House with George doing most of the talking, Faro wondered if the others were hating him as much as Poppy and himself.

CHAPTER ELEVEN

In retrospect, for Faro, there was an idyllic quality about that sunny afternoon, a moment lived out of time, neither past nor present, simply a moment of magic emanating from his Red House experience, an interlude that seemed to have the power to invent a time and place of its own, regardless of the busy world outside. A world of movement, of trains passing by in a dreamlike landscape and an oasis away from terror, danger and death.

It was also a time of self-examination, of discovery.

As they returned to Red House, preparations for the pre-wedding masque were in full swing. It was to have, as would have been expected, a medieval theme relished by everyone.

There was an atmosphere of excited anticipation—the occupants had a childlike love of dressing up, adults returning to their school days, artists reliving the portraits they had created, a return to innocence that made it hard to believe that these grown-ups lived lives of intrigue, with adulterous emotions of illicit love simmering under the surface.

As Poppy gossiped to Faro, it was already obvious to everyone that newly married Janey Morris and Rossetti were in love and that was the reason his long-time model and bride of just a few months, Elizabeth Siddall, looked perpetually anxious and unhappy.

Erland told him that the two ladies were dressed as Hippolyte and Helen of Troy from Gabriel's painting of Chaucer's *Legend of Goode Women*.

'Somewhat ironic in the circumstances, isn't it?' he added in a delighted whisper.

An added excitement for the ball were the medieval dresses from Morris's overflowing costume wardrobes worn by the models, perhaps a little more shabby with wear—and occasionally spots of paint—and as it was a masked ball identities were to be strictly concealed: veiled headdresses for the ladies, crowned with leaves, replicas of Rossetti's painting of Dante's 'Beatrice in Eden'. In addition men and women alike were issued with velvet face masks, hopefully creating a new allure and mystery. Except that Faro decided the faces behind the masks would be very easy to identify, although the ladies headdresses and flowing veils made recognition a little more difficult, especially as Poppy and Lena were of similar height and colouring.

His hopes that he might quietly be overlooked in these preparations were doomed. Unsurprisingly, Topsy Morris had found a very convincing Viking costume for him: a leather doublet, leggings and a very convincing helmet complete with horns.

'This isn't the same costume as you'll be needing for Gabriel's Tarquinius.' He grinned. 'We thought it would be more comfortable than a warrior's armoured breastplate, but not so dramatic.'

As Faro contemplated the result in his bedroom cheval mirror, he had little faith in the velvet mask concealing his identity. He realised that his suggestion to Erland of paying for his board and lodgings had been taken advantage of by the artists. He would have much preferred putting his hand in his pocket and handing over the few guineas rent involved, he guessed that Morris and company did not require.

Considerable thought and lavish preparations for the masque had been taking place behind the kitchen doors, hinting that money did not seem to be in short supply whereas male models certainly were. His only hope was delaying tactics, that he might be summoned back to Edinburgh before he was summoned to Rossetti's studio.

For convenience, the round table had been replaced by long trestles to accommodate the guests, the banquet complete with roast pig, numerous fowls, fish in the shape of salmon and a variety of shellfish, Morris's special delicacy ordered and delivered that day. All were presented with a lavish display of vegetables from the gardens, always ready at hand, served in several different sauces and relishes with an assortment of excellent wines from the Red House cellars.

As a final dash of grandeur and sense of occasion befitting a meal that might have been served at the Knight's Round Table, Morris their host, with Gabriel Rossetti, Ned Burne-Jones, their womenfolk and the principal guests (including George Wardle, conveniently seated alongside Lena and Erland) were provided with a 'squire' stationed behind their dining chair to serve them their food and wine individually.

Between courses, each preceded by an appropriate toast and eulogy in the form of a poem or reading, Morris was persuaded, not unwillingly, to deliver some readings from his own works. He chose an extract from an early draft of *The Earthly Paradise,* an epic poem, he explained apologetically, that he was engaged on at present.

A respectful hush descended on the assembled diners as his sonorous voice proclaimed:

'Dreamer of dreams, born out of my due time
Why should I strive to set the crooked
    straight?
Love is enough, though the world be a-waning,
And the woods have no voice but the voice of
    complaining.'

In the applause that followed Faro decided that there must be a message for more than one of those present. As if the thought had also struck Poppy, she whispered, 'In the absence of a minister, that was a kind of grace before meals, almost a prayer, wasn't it?'

And Faro, remembering her passionate response to his kisses, had no voice for complaining. The message was clear. Glancing at Poppy, he touched her hand; love was enough. Let the evening take him where it would.

While the meal continued, from the musicians' gallery, a worthy addition to the dining room, they were serenaded by some enthusiastic but amateur performers. These were, Faro guessed, local residents, their shortcomings lost in the loud conversations, particularly from their host, whose voice got louder as did his roars of laughter as the evening progressed and the wine store diminished.

As the squires paid due attention to the needs of the guests, Faro recognised among them some of the gardeners who had been recruited for this purpose and suitably adorned in medieval costume. To his embarrassment, he was certain that he recognised his personal squire as one of the lads he had asked about Bess Tracy's whereabouts and later he wondered if he had imagined that fleeting, knowing look, now observing him with a somewhat clinging Poppy.

He could not, however, mistake another knowing look and one of considerable satisfaction from Erland seated opposite, obviously delighted that matters between Faro and Poppy were moving in what he considered the right direction. He did not seem to observe that George Wardle was completely monopolising Lena, who did not seem to mind in the least.

Wardle was the only one of the assembled guests who had refused to wear a medieval costume, but had been persuaded into a medieval lawyer's dark robe complete with eye mask. It did not diminish his appeal as Lena appeared to hang upon every whispered word, laughing and smiling up at him.

As the meal progressed, and sampling all dishes but avoiding the shellfish to which he was allergic from his Orkney days, Faro thought fleetingly of staid dining tables in far off Edinburgh's New Town society in their Georgian houses. And as an evening like this was never likely to occur again, remembering the passionate but sadly brief interlude with Poppy at the picnic that afternoon, with each refill of his goblet he resolutely banished all thoughts of being faithful to the absent Lizzie. Their relationship so far was limited to chaste goodnight kisses, his experience of sex and the rapture of first love still untouched from his early days in Orkney with Inga St Ola.

He glanced quickly at Poppy. Was that who she reminded him of? Those lost rapturous days. Certainly there was a distinct resemblance between the two passionate women. As for his Lizzie, he had to admit she was pretty enough, but on reflection he doubted that she would thrill and excite him as a lover. He acknowledged that she failed to stir his senses as did his first love and now Poppy.

Poppy and Lizzie were of a similar age yet could not have been more different and he suspected that, even though Lizzie had borne a child, she had much less experience of men than the vivacious girl at his side. Perhaps the shocking circumstances of Vince's birth had made Lizzie extra cautious of any display of passion. Bearing this in mind, Faro was extremely careful to exercise self-control and never scare her off.

Poppy's goblet replenished once again, she moved closer and smiled tenderly up at him. As their heads came momentarily close together, he was aware of an argument behind him between his squire and his opposite number, the squire across the table where Erland and Lena were sitting.

Faro could hardly distinguish the words through the noise of conversation and the drift of music from above their heads, but he caught small phrases: 'Who do you think—who told you—no mask . . .'

He could make nothing of the altercation but turning in his chair he saw that his squire, unlike those across the table in his line of vision, was wearing a velvet mask which had apparently upset the other squire.

But Erland was demanding his attention. Flourishing the wine bottle, he said tipsily, 'Never mind the argument. My friend over there has lost his goblet. Get him another— meanwhile,' he hiccuped, 'I want Jeremy to drink a toast to us. Here's mine.'

Lena smiled, slid the goblet across the table and offered Erland her own, Faro's to remain untouched. Both hands were needed at that moment to applaud their host as Morris took the floor once more and delivered another lengthy epistle, its content lost upon most of the assembled company, some of whom were already fast asleep at the table.

Polite applause and cheers followed, goblets were raised in more toasts to absent friends and artists. Faro stretched out his hand, but Erland's goblet was no longer in front of him, its place was empty.

Deciding it had been removed by one of the squires, he called for another. This did not seem significant until much later when even through a wine mist Faro returned to that incident in absolute clarity. His exceptional memory and gift of total recall was to be of considerable importance in retrospect. Then he was prepared to swear that Lena, handing Erland her own goblet, had watched him carefully as he drank the contents. Moments later, or so it seemed, Erland stood up abruptly, swayed and almost fell, recovered and headed towards the door.

Everyone laughed. Too bad, too much to drink!

Lena rose and followed him out. When they did not return, Faro, suddenly sobered, whispered to Poppy that he needed to go outside, the excuse to relieve himself.

The sharp night air cleared his head momentarily, he lingered for a while under that star-filled sky, the trees around him shimmering, rustling, silvered in moonlight. Somewhere a village clock solemnly struck four. The night was almost over. Soon it would be the dawn of another day, and thankfully as it was Sunday, he would be spared a visit to Constable Muir. He wondered cynically whether villains like Macheath were aware of this convenient rest day and the opportunities it offered.

Reluctant to leave the peaceful garden and return to the raucous noise within the dining room, he saw that the places Erland and Lena had occupied were still empty.

Gazing upon the scene, he wondered how he could extract Poppy from an animated conversation with Gabriel who, circulating among the guests, was leaning over her chair. Was she arranging their next sitting, he wondered as, back in the hall, apart from frantic voices and busy sounds emanating from the kitchen area, the rest of the house seemed strangely quiet.

Indecisively he lingered, the idea of more food and forced merriment suddenly abhorrent. Climbing the stairs none too steadily, his senses telling him that he was to pay dearly for the effects of all that wine, bed was the only sensible alternative.

Halfway upstairs, he leant on the banister, listening to the quiet. It seemed likely that Erland and Lena had decided that they had also had more than enough of the banquet and had retired to Erland's room.

He would have liked to know the outcome of Erland's hasty departure from the dining table and that all was now well with him but could hardly intrude on them. Nevertheless, he was unable to rid himself of a growing anxiety, a feeling that something was wrong.

Suddenly he heard his name.

Erland was sitting alone in the shadows at the curve of the staircase overhead. Faro ran up to him. 'Where's Lena?'

'Gone to bed.' Erland groaned. He put his hands to his head. 'Dear God, Jeremy—I feel awful.'

In a wavering gesture he grasped Faro's hand, his own cold and clammy for all the warm atmosphere. 'I've never felt as bad as this before. I feel as if—as if I'm going to die,' he whispered.

Faro regarded him anxiously. There was little light in the ensconced candles but enough to see that Erland certainly looked ill, pale and sweating as if in the grip of a fever.

Consolingly Faro said, 'Too much wine, I'm afraid. That's what's wrong with you. I don't feel any too good myself. There'll be sore heads all round tomorrow.'

'That's it—the wine.' Erland rallied with effort. 'Don't usually feel this bad though. Must be a bad batch. Hope Lena's all right.' He shuddered. 'Feel as if—as if I've been poisoned.'

At those words, so ominous to Faro, with a groan he sank his head in his hands again. 'Thankfully I've managed to vomit most of it out of my system. I think my stomach must be quite empty now.' He stood up shakily leaning for support against the banister.

'Are you going to be all right?' Faro asked.

Straightening up with effort, Erland said, 'I think so. I'm for bed. Lena'll be asleep by now. I'll try not to disturb her.' Smiling weakly, his legs seemed shaky and Faro helped him to the bedroom door.

Faro hovered anxiously. 'Do you need any help?'

Erland, shaking his head, whispered, 'No. Thank you, old chap. Lena will tuck me in.'

Faro remained outside the closed door, listening.

There was no sound of voices and he walked slowly back to his own room, wishing Erland hadn't mentioned the word poison. Knowing what he did, the scene at the dining table of Lena handing Erland her goblet returned vividly to him, his thoughts coldly reviewing it in minute detail.

But why should Lena poison Erland, who she had agreed to marry in two days' time? Then he knew there was one very good reason indeed.

For Madeleine Smith and Emile L'Angelier versus William Minnoch read instead Lena and Erland versus George Wardle.

What had Erland Flett, a crippled and impoverished artist relying on the hospitality and generous nature of the Pre-Raphaelites, to offer her compared to George Wardle? Wardle seated by her side at the table and paying her lavish attentions, which she seemed to be fully appreciating. Wardle, a rich man like Minnoch who could elevate her to a higher position in society beyond Erland's possibilities.

And any woman might have been tempted, for most Faro knew relied on the prospect of a good marriage to see them comfortably through life. From the moment they were born, that was dinned into them by their parents and so it had been since time began.

A rich husband was life's goal. There was no other way, for that was what society demanded. And, in the case of many sad marriages, once wed a woman lost all independence. She and all her possessions became the sole property of her husband.

As he headed towards his door, his somewhat unsteady progress warned Faro of an approaching headache of mammoth proportions.

Suddenly a figure moved out of the shadows. A drift of perfume, which he did not immediately recognise, a woman's hand soft and gentle on his arm. Too dark to see her distinctly.

Remembering his promise. 'Poppy,' he whispered.

Opening his bedroom door, she led the way inside and closed the door. In the thin moonlight from the high windows, she helped him out of the Viking costume and they lay down on the bed together. He took her in his arms, her kisses deeper, even more passionate than those of the afternoon picnic, which seemed worlds away. There was no doubt in Faro's wine-muddled mind of the rapture of fulfilment that lay ahead—

It was not to be.

A tap on the door.

He heard it, cursing that there were no locks on the doors.

Again.

He couldn't ignore it. What if it was Erland needing help?

Springing out of bed he opened the door.

A smiling girl, holding a candle, stretching out her hand to him.

'You promised—so here I am,' she whispered.

'Poppy!'

Then who—

He glanced over his shoulder. The woman in his bed—

Dear God—

The woman he was making love to—

She was Madeleine Smith.

CHAPTER TWELVE

One clear thought sobered him. Somehow he had to get rid of Poppy without her seeing Lena. How had he made that appalling mistake? True, the two were alike enough and wearing almost identical costumes. It was Poppy he was expecting in his room, a pale moon its only illumination; he had been too drunk, too eager. Now he would pay dearly for that mistake.

Apologising, he told Poppy he was very tired, aware of her bewilderment, her hurt expression as she whispered that was all right, she just wanted to stay with him.

Her meaning was clear, all too clear. He shook his head and said, 'Sorry—tomorrow.'

Still not understanding, she stood on tiptoe, kissed his cheek, said bravely, 'Well then, sleep well. Goodnight—what's left of it.'

He nodded, closed the door. Leant against it weakly. There was dawn light in the sky now, the moon had gone. Somewhere nature stirred, and a cock crowed.

How appropriate, he thought grimly. That ancient sound of betrayal. How well it fitted this situation.

Lena was sitting on the bed half-dressed, unperturbed, smiling. As if this was a great joke, something to laugh about.

He looked down at her, said, 'Please go.'

Again she smiled. 'Very well. What a shame—'

'A shame indeed,' he said angrily, longing at that moment to strike her, to take away that look of amused satisfaction. 'Erland is my friend—and, in case you have forgotten, about to be your husband.' He paused, said heavily, 'You tricked me.'

'I did not. You were eager enough.'

'You tricked me,' he repeated. 'You pretended to be Poppy.'

She laughed unconcerned, unashamed. 'I never did.'

'You did.' He was coldly sober now.

She shrugged. 'You don't want me to stay.'

'I certainly do not.' He wanted to add, even if you were not Erland's woman you would be the last one in the world, knowing what I know about you, that I'd want to make love to. But remembering those kisses, that brief interlude he would never be able to forget, he knew that wasn't true.

Suddenly words were inadequate. He said again, 'Please go. Erland is ill. He needs you.' She rose from the bed, shrugged and, gathering her costume, walked out of the room without another word.

Faro also walked out, out of the house into the cool misty dawn of another day and into the woodland that skirted the Brettle's property. Birds sang a muted chorus above his

117

head, a robin added its plaintive sweet melancholy notes and with a fallen branch he struck the hedgerows, working off his rage, scared animals scuttled into their protective depths, their alarm no doubt increased by a rifle shot nearby.

The shot was so close that Faro also turned, alarmed, shouted a warning 'Hello!'

There was no reply. No doubt a farmer out shooting rabbits, although that single shot puzzled him.

Instant success, perhaps, or a poacher in the shape of Jim Boone discreetly remaining unseen. He walked on.

The enormity of last night's events was already unreal, a nightmare from which he knew there was no happy awakening. Erland must never know what happened, that he had been betrayed by his best friend, his proudly called cousin and his beloved bride-to-be.

The question remained unanswered. Why had Lena tricked him? Was it only devilment, realising that Poppy, her so-called best friend, was falling in love with him? That had to be the reason. He could not believe that in those few short days, involved entirely with preparations for her marriage to Erland, she had any affection for him. It would have made more sense if she had tried to seduce the very willing Wardle.

How long or where he walked he had little idea but somehow he walked off his anger. At last, marshalling his fears and mistakes into some sort of order as his profession had taught him, he found his true self again.

Hungry and certainly sober now, sober as perhaps he had never been before in the light of what had driven him from the house, he knew that unless Lena was a gossip, and considering her background she had doubtless learnt discretion, he guessed he would be safe enough.

The truth must be kept from Erland. As for Poppy, he was certain he could deal with that situation. At this delicate stage of their relationship, she would not jeopardise its future by asking any probing questions. He was sure that she would accept his rather lame explanation about being tired, certain that she did not know of Lena's presence in his bedroom, unless she could have seen beyond him into the room, the rumpled bed with its occupant.

As for Erland, Faro doubted that he would have felt fit enough to go in search of Lena. Hopefully he must have tumbled into bed and fallen asleep immediately, regardless of her absence.

All that remained was for him to forget everything that had happened with Lena and return to normality, or what existed as normality in Red House, rising like a fairy-tale fantasy from the morning mist.

The short-cut back led, by a back gate,

through the orchard. One of the gardeners was there, a branch breaking, the glimpse of a hooded cape. Odd, since this was their day off and considering last night's activities most would be glad not to get up at the crack of dawn. Presumably this one, anxious not to be seen, had an ulterior purpose and was out gathering a few illicit apples. He could not imagine why, for surely no one in Red House would deny him that.

Voices, a door opened and some of the dogs tumbled out for their morning walk. Janey and Georgie emerged and as he approached he thought they were also looking the worse for wear although they greeted him cheerfully enough.

'You're about early,' said Georgie and, calling her spaniels to heel as they bounded towards him, she laughed. 'Come, dogs, Mr Faro's too frail for your attentions at this hour.'

'The men are still at breakfast,' said Janey, paler than usual.

'We might feel more like it after a brisk walk,' said Georgie, 'although I feel bed would be a better bet.'

As they disappeared in the direction of the orchard gate, Faro went indoors. The dining room, its temporary trestles removed, the round table restored, still looked considerably dishevelled, its sole occupants Morris and Ned Burne-Jones.

The smell of fried sausages and bacon did nothing for Faro's well-being and he hurried upstairs to see if Erland had recovered. Tapping on the door he heard his voice and going in saw that he was still abed, Lena seated at the window.

'How are you—I see you've missed breakfast.'

Erland groaned and said faintly, 'At this moment I don't feel I ever want to eat anything ever again.'

As Faro went closer he realised that Erland looked far from well, his face yellow and jaundiced.

'I still feel awful, Jeremy. Really awful.'

'I think you should stay in bed today.' This from Lena.

Faro avoided any eye contact with her and realised that he was going to have to practise this as well as avoiding her as much as he could.

'Would you like something to drink, some coffee, perhaps?' he asked.

'No, thanks. Lena brought me some cocoa.'

Cocoa—Madeleine Smith. The connection riveted Faro as Erland said, 'Too sweet. It's left me very thirsty though—could I have some water?'

Lena stood up.

'No,' said Faro without looking at her. 'You stay here. I'll get it.' And seizing the cocoa cup as he went downstairs staring into its depths, one of the maids appeared from the kitchen with a tray and, giving him a curious look, said: 'Finished with that, sir? I'll take it.'

In answer he clutched the cup firmly, shook his head. Holding it up to the light, wondering desperately how he was to find some method of analysing the dregs, a voice behind him said a very shaky, 'Good morning.'

It was Elizabeth Siddal, carrying a tray. She looked even worse than the two women out walking their dogs.

He murmured a good morning in reply and, as she made to walk past him, she noticed the cup he was clutching and put out her hand. 'I'm going to the kitchen.'

He could hardly refuse; there was no reasonable excuse he could offer for retaining an empty cup of cocoa.

Following her downstairs, cursing to himself that this was the only evidence he might ever have, he went into the dining room and helped himself to coffee, no longer hungry and revolted by the sight of Morris gobbling down an enormous platter of poached eggs, his usual breakfast. Invited to have some, Faro declined with a shudder.

'Good for you. Hair of the dog and that sort of thing.'

Faro thought that referred to the wine only as Morris asked: 'Talking of which, how is poor old Erland this morning?'

'He's not at all well. In fact he looks bad and

I really think you should call a doctor to have a look at him.'

'A doctor?' Morris exclaimed as if Faro had asked for the man in the moon. 'What on earth would a doctor do?' And flourishing his fork at the empty table: 'Look around you, Jeremy. Where are they all this morning? Well, I'll give you a hint. Practically everyone else is suffering the same symptoms, but soldiering on very bravely,' he added piously, resuming his onslaught on the eggs.

Faro said slowly, 'I believe Erland may have been poisoned . . .'

Morris nodded. 'Yes, I believe you. It was those damned mussels to blame. Janey was very poorly during the night and so was Ned. How about you?' he asked anxiously. 'Were you all right?'

'I avoid mussels, always have done.' He had been very ill after eating some in his childhood Orkney days and had never been tempted to repeat the experience.

'Wise man. They must have been a bit off and that's what upset Erland. But poisoned—I say, that's a bit of an exaggeration, isn't it?' he added with a hearty guffaw.

'We can hardly call the doctor,' said Ned, reaching for the coffee pot.

'And it's Sunday, don't forget. All the good folk, and that includes the doctor, off to church,' Morris reminded him.

'Don't people ever get sick on Sunday?' said

123

Faro somewhat impatiently.

They both looked at him in astonishment. Obviously they thought he was making a great fuss about nothing and there was no way he could explain his anxiety. That Lena Hamilton was Madeleine Smith who had poisoned her lover in Glasgow three years ago and for reasons yet unknown but, he suspected, might have something to do with the attentions being paid her by Morris's new business manager, George Wardle, had decided to get rid of Erland Flett.

Morris was frowning at him, clearly mystified. 'We don't have much faith in doctors, Jeremy,' he said sternly. 'We find we can treat most things with natural means, like herbs. Besides we're all very healthy. Isn't that so, Ned?'

Ned thus appealed to, coughed apologetically. 'We men are pretty sturdy, y'know. Can't afford the luxury of being ill. The ladies have someone in town and we can summon him down in an emergency.'

And Faro decided those grim words might describe the situation exactly as Morris said:

'Don't worry about your cousin. A day's rest and he'll be fine. Has to be fit. Have to get him up and carry him to the altar if necessary, tomorrow—plans all made and that sort of thing,' he added with a hearty chuckle. 'More coffee?'

Faro declined and taking a carafe of water

124

went upstairs to Erland again.

Lena was still there, sitting by his bedside, a damp cloth dabbing at his forehead.

'Some water,' said Faro pushing her aside.

Erland sat up, drank greedily.

'Are you feeling any better?'

Erland did not need to shake his head to deny that. He did not look at all well. In fact he looked a lot worse.

'I don't think I'll get up today, if you don't mind, darling,' This to Lena and seizing her hand, 'Have to get better—be fit—for tomorrow.'

Lena smiled. 'You just stay in bed. I'll look after you.'

Erland nodded wearily. 'I'm so tired. I just want to sleep.'

And so Faro left them. Returning to his own room he met Morris and George Wardle emerging from the studio in earnest conversation. Two men with strong stomachs he decided, remembering with a shudder that enormous dish of poached eggs that, judging by his non-appearance at the breakfast table, had also been beyond the digestion of the business manager.

Closing his bedroom door, Faro had made up his mind. He had come to a decision—if Erland was no better by evening then whatever the whims and practices of the inhabitants of Red House, he was going in search of a doctor.

Constable Muir or Mrs Lunn at Brettle

Manor would surely know a doctor and where to find him.

CHAPTER THIRTEEN

To make matters worse, the morning mist turned into rain, a steady downpour with low skies, heavy and grey; it looked set in for the day. It fitted the mood within the house, echoing emptily as the occupants kept to their rooms to recover in their various ways from the effects of the banquet and the dubious shellfish.

Faro was not convinced about the mussels, however, but decided to opt out of any chance meeting with Poppy. He was not a good liar. Could she or anyone else for that matter be credited with accepting the truth—that he had been tricked into making love to her best friend Lena, who was also his best friend's bride-to-be, on the eve of their wedding?

He did not think so. Even if, as he suspected and had been told, Poppy was falling in love with him, then she would certainly feel hurt and rejected, especially after the promise of the afternoon's romantic interlude.

Anxious not to encounter Poppy or anyone else, he remained in his room leaving merely for a quick glance at Erland to see how he was progressing. Lena had remained true to her

126

promise and was seated in an armchair at his bedside reading a book.

When Faro entered she looked up and although she assured him that there was an improvement since morning, Faro was very doubtful. If appearances were anything to go by, he decided that it was either his anxiety or Erland's condition had definitely deteriorated.

'He is asleep,' said Lena as Faro bent over the bed for a closer look at the pale face on the pillow. 'He sleeps most of the time.'

When Faro shook his head doubtfully, she said, 'No need for you to worry about him, Jeremy. Sleep is the best possible cure, you'll see,' she added with a tender smile in Erland's direction.

Faro looked at her, so calm in his presence. The devoted nurse at her lover's bedside. It was as if last night had never happened.

Avoiding her eyes, he said stiffly, 'If you have things to do, I will stay with him.'

She shook her head, turned to look at Erland. 'Thank you, but no. It is best that I remain. He is used to having me around and he'll want to see me here when he wakes up.'

Faro followed her gaze. If he ever wakes up, he thought, fighting back the gnawing anxiety induced by that heavy, somehow unnatural slumber. As if he was drugged. Yes, that's what he looked like.

'Haven't you matters to deal with for tomorrow—for the wedding?' he reminded her bitterly.

She shrugged as if remembering it for the first time, an event of no importance. 'Tomorrow? Oh yes. All is arranged. Poppy will take care of everything—of anything that I've overlooked. But all will be well by tomorrow,' she added with a dreamy smile.

'I hope you still have a congregation.' And a bridegroom, he thought silently.

'We are only expecting a few friends.'

'And most of them are laid low with food poisoning, rotten mussels, according to our host.'

'Oh they will all be fine, I'm sure.' She smiled up at him and Faro shook his head, saying coldly, 'I hope you're right.'

'Oh, I always am.'

He could take no more of Lena and made his way back to his room. How was he to fill in the rest of the day, which promised to be unending with rain lashing down the windows?

Closing the door, he thought of his old ally Inspector McFie and on an impulse he wrote him a letter that would be awaiting his return home after his holiday in Sussex.

Telling him briefly of his frustration over Macheath and the daily reports to Noble, adding that he longed to return to Edinburgh, he ended briefly that he had encountered 'MS'.

'She is now living a life of luxury here in Red House using a different name and in curious circumstances, about to marry an old school friend from Orkney.'

He would have liked to say more, but he never found writing letters an easy task. His letters tended to be terse and brief and, on this occasion, he felt unable to find the right words to explain his emotions regarding Lena Hamilton's deception.

Sealing the letter he turned next to his logbook, now containing a record of his daily visits to the police office, which in due course must be presented to Noble to justify any additional expenses although the money he had been given was still more or less untouched thanks to the hospitality at Red House.

He threw down the pen with an exclamation of annoyance and frustration. What he had written concerning his daily routine sounded even worse than his letter to McFie, the account of a hopeless quest and a complete waste of time.

There was a lot he wished to add to his logbook, in particular the unexpected meeting with Madeleine Smith, but as that had nothing to do with his pursuit and recapture of Macheath, he decided to write it up separately.

Removing a page, he headed it with the possible poisoning attempt on Erland Flett and the scenes he had witnessed at the dining table regarding his own missing goblet of wine.

Was this a coincidence, Erland's severe

sickness due to the mussels he had eaten which had also given several of the other diners minor symptoms of food poisoning? Or was he deliberately poisoned in the course of the banquet, the obvious way, the still tried and true method used by murderers throughout the ages?

In the wine. Who then could have put poison in Erland's goblet?

He had been seated next to Lena and George Wardle. George Wardle seemed an unlikely suspect. Although his infatuation for Lena was quite evident, Faro could hardly believe that he was the kind of man who would risk all by poisoning his rival at William Morris's table.

And that left Lena. The business he had witnessed with the goblet still troubled him. Seeing Lena hand Erland her own, watching him drink it.

Remembering the altercation between the two gardeners in their roles of squires, one stationed behind Erland's chair and the other, masked, behind his own, created another picture, another mystery. Did it concern the goblet Erland had passed over to him which had vanished?

Again there had to be a motive. Too obscure to be credible was that the gardener was in league with Wardle or with Lena. And he was suddenly alert to another highly improbable interpretation. What if—what if it was he who had been the intended victim, and the missing goblet with its poison, had been passed to Erland by mistake.

This idea raised the vital question. Who in Red House would want him dead? His identity as a policeman was unknown except by Erland—and perhaps by Lena. Was there a possibility that she recognised him from her trial as Madeleine Smith and feared for her reputation with the revelation of the fabrications she had invented when she became the artist's protégée? She had no other reason to wish him dead, considering her amorous behaviour later that evening.

But in spite of this speculation, he must not forget that there was one other person who desired his death. And that was Macheath. However, the idea of him stalking Red House awaiting an opportunity instead of remaining safely hidden in the depths of London was too ludicrous for serious consideration.

Returning to Lena, she was still the strongest suspect. If she had intended to poison Erland then luck and opportunity were certainly with her, the perfect alibi provided by the bad batch of mussels that had wreaked havoc among some of the other diners.

If this was so, then one vital question remained unanswered. Where had she got the poison from? It was unlikely that she kept a ready supply of arsenic in her packet of cocoa and if she had purchased it locally, then she must have signed a pharmacy book. The other possibility was the existence of an accomplice, a gardener who had unquestioned access to arsenic for killing rats.

Again he came to motives. If Lena had poisoned Erland, she had one undeniable and very strong reason. The advent of George Wardle. On the very eve of her wedding, a wealthy man of property with high social connections had, according to Poppy, asked Lena to marry him when they met a few days earlier in London during their shopping expedition.

Was this good enough reason to repeat the Madeleine Smith procedure and get rid of her husband-to-be who could never hope to keep her in such fashion or in any kind of luxury once removed from the shelter and hospitality of their generous host in Red House?

Emile L'Angelier could no longer be held against her. She had been tried for his murder and the jury had returned Scotland's 'Not Proven'; a third verdict, returned when insufficient evidence exists for conviction and the defendant is unconditionally discharged, had saved her from the gallows.

She could not be re-tried for the same crime.

But should anything happen to Erland, should he die, Faro resolved grimly, then he would make quite sure that her second try would not be so fortunate under English law.

This time she would hang.

CHAPTER FOURTEEN

As he left his room, walking across the landing, Rossetti poked his head around his studio door. 'Recovered from last night? No ill effects? Good, good.'

Obviously no replies were expected. Rossetti had a sketchbook under his arm. He smiled. 'The very man I was hoping to find. If you have a few minutes to spare—not intending to go anywhere in this shocking weather, were you?'

And before Faro could respond, he went on rapidly, 'Good, good,' and flourishing a piece of charcoal, 'Time for a few preliminary sketches before I embark on the rape painting. Come in, come in.'

As Faro followed him into the studio, he realised the moment of truth could no longer be delayed. He was to pay for his hospitality.

Rossetti pointed to the raised dais. 'Over there, if you please. Lean against the draped chair.'

Faro looked at the chair and hesitated. 'I am afraid I have no experience—' he began, trying to explain, hoping for a loophole of escape.

'No experience needed.' The artist laughed. 'Not a bit of it. You just have to pose like this.' And standing up he demonstrated what appeared to Faro to be a somewhat threatening attitude. 'There now. Just be yourself. This won't hurt!'

Faro did as he was told, feeling foolish and self-conscious as, without another word, Rossetti bent his head over the paper and, narrowing his eyes and pursing his lips, he studied Faro intently.

A moment later he held up the charcoal and sighed. Faro's hopes that he was to be released were doomed as the artist shook his head. 'You are a little overclad for a warrior, my friend. But first things first.'

Faro blenched at the prospect of removing his clothes. This was a new role. Nothing like that had ever happened in the Edinburgh City Police, or so he believed. All his colleagues were either young bachelors or middle-aged married men who seemed quite old. He had never let his mind dwell on what they looked like without their uniforms and it was beyond imagination to visualise any of them standing on the artist's plinth, naked. Nakedness in public or, he suspected, in private was not rife in the strata of society in which he lived although rumour had it that in some of those private Edinburgh gentlemen's clubs, clients could for an exorbitant fee get rid of their inhibitions, inhibitions which included their clothes as many a police raid on houses of ill-repute revealed.

He wasn't listening to Rossetti who talked as he drew. He forced himself to concentrate on what was being said.

'Really appreciate this, Faro. Most of our chaps have been well used in all our historic depictions of ancient times. Not great figures by any means but well covered up, cloaks and capes, drapery and a bit of imagination.'

He sighed, flourishing the charcoal with satisfaction. 'Ah yes, you have certain advantages. Being so tall, you have a certain style and elegance.' And narrowing his eyes, 'Well made, muscular, d'you know you definitely remind me of those models Leonardo da Vinci drew . . .' An appreciative sigh. 'Those pectoral muscles—quite exceptional. Just wish Topsy could see 'em.'

Faro shuddered at the prospect of being on display. The anonymity of a respectable policeman shattered—what would Edinburgh City Police think of that da Vinci description?

'Now turn your head—profile! Yes, yes, fine classical features too. Where did you say you were from? Orkney, wasn't it? Remarkable, remarkable. Thank God you haven't become a slave of fashion, and the present weakness we men have for facial hair.' Grinning, he stroked his own beard. 'Afraid we're all a bit lazy, beards are so handy and time-saving, but alas, not elegant. Having a model who is clean-shaven will be a great advantage.' He sighed. 'Just for a change, I can see the bone structure of the man I'm painting.'

Pausing he stared critically at his easel,

135

frowning, lips pursed. 'Yes, I can see Tarquinius emerging, and Poppy as Lucrece—perfect together! And by God, even another epic I have always had in mind. Jacob and the Angel. Remember the Bible story?'

A shake of the head. 'Alas, you're too young for Jacob with his two wives and umpteen children, not a very worthy or admirable character either; he cheated his brother. You look too honest,' he said regretfully. 'Not nearly sly enough.'

Faro had a fleeting shiver as he remembered how last night had almost ended by cheating Erland with Lena as Rossetti went on.

'One of the girls for the angel. Lena perhaps or Janey Morris,' and pausing to look at the rain streaming down the windows, 'Well, there is no time like the present.'

This situation was getting worse but it could not be avoided. This rent for bed and board at Red House was cheap at the price of such a luxury. To try to get out of this request for a model even if he could think of a valid excuse might also suggest that there was some truth in the well-kenned adage that the Scots were mean by nature. And for anyone hazy about the geography of Britain, that would undoubtedly include the far northern race of Orcadians too.

Rossetti continued to sketch rapidly for a few minutes in silence. As he threw down his charcoal with a smile, Faro sighed deeply. The session was at an end, escape at last. But that was not to be.

'Face complete, that will do. Now I need neck and shoulders. If you don't mind removing your upper garments—that would be a tremendous help. It won't take long,' he added reassuringly.

Faro did as he was bid and Rossetti produced from a trunk alongside a sword and a scarlet robe. 'Drape this about your shoulder. Hold the sword. That's right.' Frowning he regarded the result. 'Ah, yes, there's something missing. Legs!' he shouted triumphantly. 'Of course, Roman warriors had bare legs.' A wheedling smile. 'If you don't mind, old chap.'

And so it was that Faro found himself standing in his underdrawers, flourishing the sword and feeling far from warrior-like as Rossetti sketched. After a few minutes, he sighed and said apologetically: 'Do you think you could possibly look a little menacing? Try to imagine there is a beautiful woman lying naked on that couch, you are a conqueror.' He coughed, muttered, 'Do think some lustful thoughts, old chap. You are to take a woman against her will and love every minute of it.'

A look at Faro's startled countenance and he said wearily, 'Never mind—we'll get round to that later once we have Poppy or one of the girls here. I'm sure we can then achieve the necessary result.'

Some time later, it seemed like hours rather

than minutes, Rossetti looked round from his easel and said, 'Take a break now, old chap. Finished for the day.'

Curious to view the result, Faro asked, 'May I see?'

In answer, Rossetti threw up his hands in horror and swiftly turned the easel away. 'Not allowed, old chap, sorry. Never show a portrait at this stage.' He smiled. 'I must compliment you on being a remarkably good model. You have tremendous poise and serenity. An admirable stillness that few beginners ever achieve. They soon get weary, shifting about from foot to foot, complaining of cramps—'

Faro considered that compliment remarkable as he had felt extremely uncomfortable throughout as Rossetti went on, 'If you ever want a job down here as a model, you have only to ask, you know.'

Getting dressed again in his outer garments, Faro felt suddenly weary. A sudden uneasy thought. What if anyone in Edinburgh ever saw him in Rossetti's painting?

He shuddered. He would never live that one down. Fame as an artist's male model would not look well in his references and indeed would be regarded with suspicion in any suggestion of promotion in the ranks of the Edinburgh City Police. He could hear his colleagues chortle, their bawdy remarks. The only fame he longed for lay in achieving his eventual goal as a detective inspector. He firmly believed that success in apprehending Macheath would provide the first step on the ladder and being a male model for the famous Pre-Raphaelites was a notoriety he could do without.

*   *   *

Downstairs in the dining room he was informed by the maids that a set midday meal had been abandoned and, should he wish for a tray in his room, sandwiches and soup would be sent up to him—a welcome alternative to being surrounded by diners strong enough to emerge from their rooms and take a little light nourishment, happy to regale others with their horrible symptoms.

Afterwards he made another visit to Erland and realised that despite Lena's continued assurances that all would be well by tomorrow, he was amazed that she refused to recognise that Erland's condition had deteriorated. Unable to rouse him, Faro called upon Morris who again made light of his demands that a doctor be summoned immediately, assuring him that his anxiety was unfounded.

Aware that argument with Lena or with Morris was useless he would wait no longer. He would take the matter into his own hands.

Hoping to keep out of Poppy's way after last night's events, they met on the stairs and so there was no avoiding this encounter. A polite and rather stiff exchange of greetings and she asked, 'You are quite well?'

When he responded in the affirmative, she said, 'I gather you avoided the shellfish too. Very fortunate. Lena tells me poor Erland has not been so fortunate.'

'I am very concerned about him. I'm going for a doctor.'

She raised her eyebrows in amazement. 'Is that really necessary? Lena has been with him all night, she says he is on the mend and will be well enough for the wedding tomorrow.' Frowning, she added, 'It will be a tragedy if it has to be cancelled or postponed.'

Convinced by Lena's assurances, this was Poppy's main concern and as Faro was unable to confide his suspicions regarding the true cause of Erland's indisposition, he asked for the local doctor's address.

She shook her head. 'Ask Topsy. He probably knows of someone, but we are all pretty healthy here.'

'So he tells me.'

Quickly changing the subject, Poppy smiled. 'What are you planning to do this evening?' she asked hopefully.

'I rather think I am going to be somewhat busy.'

And without further explanation, he bowed and left her looking sadly after him as he returned to his room. A glance at the streaming windows confirmed the necessity of some protection against the weather.

He was sorry to disappoint Poppy but at that moment he could think of nothing but the urgency of finding a doctor for Erland. The wedding tomorrow was the least of his worries.

He ducked out of sight, hearing voices from Erland's room. Lena emerged with George Wardle. They exchanged a brief embrace and blowing him a kiss she watched him disappear down the stairs.

This was a new turn to events. Were they both in the plot together? There was no time to lose, he felt certain that Erland's life now depended on immediate medical treatment.

Seizing a rain cape from the hall he set off into the downpour. First he would go to the local inn and summon the innkeeper who would surely know where the doctor lived.

The alehouse however was firmly closed; doubtless the owner treasured his day off as well. Faro walked round the outside but could find no private entrance so, after a further hammering on the inn door, he gave up and retreated in frustration and anger.

Constable Muir lived next to the police station and making his way to that now familiar territory, Faro decided he should have come here in the first place.

He was out of luck. There was no reply. Staring up at the windows, Faro remembered that the constable had mentioned that he and his wife were going to a family wedding in

London this weekend. So that was that. Doubtless they would not be back until late and he could not afford to linger.

Where next? The vicar perhaps? Evensong drifted across the street from the village church, but close at hand was Brettle Manor and as Faro wanted to call on Mrs Lunn again, this was the perfect excuse.

Footsteps from inside the kitchen could be heard in response to his tap on the door.

A voice called cheerfully, 'Door's open.'

He stepped inside and Mrs Lunn, who was seated at the table, turned to face him. Her welcoming smile faded quickly to be replaced by confusion as well as fear and anxiety. He was not her expected visitor.

Apologising for the intrusion, Faro explained that one of the people at Red House was ill with food poisoning and needed a doctor urgently. Did she have the doctor's address?

'You'd need to go to Upton,' she said

'Is there not a local doctor?' Faro asked, amazed.

She shrugged, giving him a curious look. 'I've no idea. Haven't the Morrises got someone?' And without waiting for a reply she went on, 'Sir and madam have their own physician— from London. He visits when necessary.'

She stood up, the indication that their short meeting was over. 'I have things to do, if you don't mind.'

As she moved in the direction of the door, he

142

said, 'This is an odd state of affairs. What if someone has an accident or takes seriously ill?'

Frowning now, clearly anxious in case that visitor she had been expecting was about to put in an appearance, she said, 'I have no idea. People just have to stay healthy, that's all—make their own arrangements, sign up with the Upton one.'

Opening the door for him, he remembered the coat rack with its burden of cloaks and shawls.

There was an addition today. One of the hooded capes worn by the Red House gardeners.

'Do you take in lodgers, Mrs Lunn?'

'What on earth makes you think that?' was the indignant response. 'Sir and madam—'

'I mean while they are away—'

'What a suggestion!'

'I just wondered. After all, with the house empty for several months, all those empty rooms. No one could blame you,' he added with a significant glance at the gardener's cape.

'I've never heard of such a thing—it's outrageous,' she stammered and then: 'Oh—that!' she gulped, 'belongs to my nephew. Comes to see me occasionally and sleeps on my sofa. Wouldn't consider intruding into the house,' she ended piously. 'Now if you'll excuse me, I have work to do.'

Faro went down the drive very thoughtfully. He was certain that the housekeeper was not telling the absolute truth, not that he blamed her for making a few extra shillings for boarding one of the Red House gardeners. However, it was none of his business, which right now was to find a doctor and take him to have a look at Erland.

He was walking along the road towards Upton when the sound of a carriage made him turn round. It was the Red House wagonette, and George Wardle leant out.

'Can we give you a lift? Going to catch the train. Jump in.'

Faro did so. Had what he witnessed with Lena been merely a polite farewell kiss?

'I see you've recovered from last night's festivities. I trust you avoided mussels too?' Wardle laughed. 'I left some very sore heads and even sorer stomachs back there. Where are you off to?'

Faro explained that he was in search of a doctor.

'You won't find one back there, I'm afraid. Is it urgent?' Wardle asked anxiously.

'I think so. For Erland—he is very poorly.'

Wardle shook his head. 'I wouldn't let that worry you too much. So are they all. By tomorrow all will be well again and wiser.'

'But this is different. Erland seems to be getting worse by the hour. And yes, I'm very concerned.'

'Of course. The wedding.' Wardle nodded slowly. 'Has to be fit for that. Topsy asked me to stay but alas I have important engagements in London. That's why I've spent the whole day with him.'

For Wardle's non-appearance at the wedding Faro was grateful as he continued, 'I do know a doctor in Upton, friend of mine from college days. I'd stop by and introduce you but haven't time. Only one evening train on Sundays, you know. However, we pass Dr Grant's house on the way to the station and we can drop you off at the very gate.'

Faro was again grateful as the wagonette deposited him outside a handsome new villa. 'Good luck. And give Freddie my best,' Wardle shouted in farewell.

Opening the gate, Faro walked up the path through the pretty garden and rang the front doorbell.

It was opened by a maid. 'The doctor is away from home, sir. He'll be back tomorrow. Can I take a message?'

Faro told her he was urgently required at Red House, as soon as possible. It was the best he could do and that she was to tell Dr Grant that Mr Wardle sent his regards.

As he was walking back down the road, he hailed the wagonette approaching on its way back to Red House. He was glad to escape the rain since he was now drenched through, even his boots oozed water. As they sped along the road, past the Mill House, he realised he had not thought for some time of the fate of Bess Tracy. There were no lights in the cottage and he wondered if she was still alive.

CHAPTER FIFTEEN

Faro left the shelter of the wagonette to find the scene at Red House dismal indeed. The orchard was hardly visible through the rain, trees dripping heavy with water, the courtyard flooded.

There were voices from the dining room as Faro deposited his rain cape on the hall stand and squelched his way upstairs, glad to get out of his wet clothes and remove his sodden boots. After drying his hair with a towel, he made his way along to Erland's room.

His approach had been anticipated for Poppy came to the door.

'He's asleep and he seems a little better.'

As he angled his way past her, she put a hand on his arm, frowning. 'Please don't disturb him, he needs all the sleep he can get. Lena has been with him all day. Hardly eaten a thing. I insisted that she go downstairs and have supper.' She smiled sadly. 'Poor Lena. I had to almost throw her out. She has refused to leave him for an instant.'

While she spoke, Faro edged nearer the bed.

146

It was too dark by the light of a solitary candle to see Erland's shadowed face clearly, difficult to see whether he looked better or worse as he was sleeping very deeply, his chest rising and falling with the effort.

'How long has he been like that?'

'Most of the day, I'm told.'

Faro sneezed and she gave him an anxious look. 'I hope you're not taking a fever. I gather,' she added with a glance at his wet hair, 'that you've been out braving this atrocious weather.'

'I won't melt away,' he said shortly. 'I've been searching for a doctor to come and look at Erland. Best I could do was leave a message for Dr Grant.'

She nodded slowly. 'Lena asked me if that was where you had gone. If he isn't any better by tomorrow, we both agreed that a doctor should be called. The others similarly afflicted have mostly recovered—to varying degrees.' She smiled wryly. 'I suspect that was according to the amount of wine consumed rather than the mussels.'

The door opened behind them and Lena appeared.

She seemed surprised to see him there and said to Poppy, 'Thank you—I'll take over now.'

Poppy pointed to the sewing on the bedside table.

'I'll keep you company.'

Lena sighed. 'At least there have been no

interruptions today. I've had plenty of time on my hands.'

'I'll fetch more candles, shall I?' And indicating what looked like a stack of velvet material thrown across a chair, Poppy added ruefully, 'We still have plenty to do.'

Lena nodded. 'No urgency now, I'm afraid.' She sighed. 'Everyone involved has been told.'

'No wedding?'

It was a question from Faro and Lena shook her head sadly. 'Alas, no.' Then looking at the sleeping figure, she brightened. 'But no matter, there will be other times for weddings,' she added wistfully.

Indeed yes, but as he was leaving, Faro wondered whether it was Erland she was thinking of at that moment?

In the dining room, he found a very much sobered group tackling cold meats with re-heated vegetables and, as befitted the survivors of last night's banquet, like the diners themselves, somewhat wilted.

Apart from a brief greeting, the wave of a fork momentarily suspended from Morris whose appetite seemed unimpaired, Faro was ignored. He had little wish to be sociable and soon realised that his presence was quite superfluous to the animated discussion between Morris, Rossetti and Burne-Jones regarding care needed in travel arrangements for their works at forthcoming exhibitions, galleries with atrocious hanging facilities as

148

well as greedy owners.

Bypassing the wine bottle headed in his direction, Faro seized the pause to mention Erland's postponed wedding. For a moment they stared at him blankly as if this was the first they had heard of it. Then, with murmurs of 'Too bad, rotten luck', returned to more important matters, a heated discussion about how to evade the hefty commissions London galleries were charging.

Faro ate his indifferent meal in silence; his departure, carrying his coffee, caused no raised heads in his direction. Halfway upstairs he met Elizabeth Siddal looking more ethereal than ever, as if a strong puff of wind might blow her away.

'Gabriel said you were anxious about your friend. That he should see a doctor. We often have stomach upsets and as it has just cause,' she smiled palely, 'wine—and other things, we don't take them very seriously. However, some of us—we ladies do have occasional medical problems, I'm afraid, although there is little sympathy,' she added with a dark glance downstairs at the closed dining-room door as if they might be overheard. 'They—believe in mind over matter. Illness is despised and depression regarded as an indulgence of one's own making.'

She was more voluble than usual and looking at her face, so beautiful and frail, he wondered how much of this was from her own bitter experience. 'We cannot wait always for our doctor from London, excellent as he is. I—and the other girls—prefer to have a doctor near at hand for our troubles. An excellent fellow, Dr Innes, lives a couple of miles down the road and I have sent one of the grooms with a message. He will come tomorrow and have a look at Erland—and give me some more of my medicine,' she whispered. 'Something we ladies prefer to keep a secret.'

Faro guessed that would be laudanum, the universal pain-killer, used by even the highest in the land, including, according to rumour, Her Majesty.

He looked in to see Erland again and, although he was very poorly, he was awake, with Lena helping him drink from a cup.

What was in it? Was it cocoa? Faro did not dare to ask.

Erland raised his head from the pillow and smiled weakly. 'So sorry, old chap.' And with a shake of his head, 'I don't think I'll be able to get married tomorrow. Awful to disappoint all my dear friends—and my precious girl here. But I feel so weak, I don't want to fall down and alarm everyone during the ceremony.'

And to Lena, 'I used to faint regularly at school but I outgrew that. Remember, Jeremy?'

Faro had almost forgotten and he had a sudden vision of those far-off days, a return to the protective affection he had known for the once frail, crippled boy as Erland reached out and seized his hand. His other hand sought Lena.

'And here I am laid low, but with my very best friend and my very best girl. Who could ask for more? You'll see me right, won't you?'

A shaft of fear, of terrible premonition, swept through Faro at this strange pronouncement. He looked at Lena, now stroking Erland's forehead. A faithful, loving and gentle nurse: hard to reconcile with the passionate woman who had come to his bed last night. He shuddered at the remembrance. At least Erland would never know of that encounter, that betrayal.

Erland's eyes had closed again. His hand released, Faro stood up and Lena, without looking at him, said, 'You go to bed, Jeremy. I will stay with him. He likes to see me when he wakes up.'

'The doctor is coming tomorrow.'

'I know. That is for the best, best not to take chances with food poisoning,' she added, in complete denial of her earlier reassurances.

*　　　*　　　*

He slept badly that night, troubled by nightmares, and left the house early next morning to call on Constable Muir, to get his farcical daily visit behind him. Not that he imagined there would have been any sightings

151

of Macheath over the weekend. Perhaps in the criminal fraternity that was giving him shelter, Macheath too could be relied upon as going to ground, untroubled by thoughts of hell and damnation being preached in sermons throughout the land, but merely taking it easy and staying out of trouble on Sunday.

The rain had stopped and a thin sunshine fingered the drenched gardens. Already the storm had stripped some of the leaves from the trees, carpeting the grass with their first red and gold.

Taking the short-cut through the orchard, Faro observed that three of the gardeners were already hard at work, three young lads chattering like magpies over their weekend exploits. He wondered if they were well paid by Morris for their roles at the banquet.

They greeted him cheerfully. He recognised one of them as Erland's squire and this was a great opportunity to get some answers from him regarding the wine. As he paused indecisively the trio stopped talking and stared at him. Unable to think of an excuse to detach the man from his comrades, Faro merely nodded and continued his walk.

As always he imagined their amused comments following him, especially after having obviously misunderstood his query regarding Bess Tracy, their giggling comments would doubtless be: 'Bet that queer cove is after a woman again.'

At the police office, Muir emerged from his cloud of smoke to give the now routine negative response about Macheath and Faro sent the usual negative telegraph to Edinburgh.

He would soon have been in Kent for a week. A wasted week but now, for the first time, he was no longer dismayed or frustrated by Noble's response, hoping that he would not be summoned back to Edinburgh before he could see Erland recovered.

When he told Muir that the wedding was postponed and the reason, the constable shrugged and said enigmatically, 'I expect they're well married already if not churched— if you get my meaning—from what I hear of the morals of the folk back yonder.'

A pause, then he grinned. 'What was your evening like—apart from the food poisoning I mean. Were there any interesting goings-on?'

Faro shook his head firmly. He had no intention of indulging Muir's low opinion of artists and gossip about their scandalous behaviour, which was rife in the district, so changing the subject, he asked, 'Any word yet of Bess Tracy returning home?'

Muir puffed energetically at his pipe. 'Haven't heard.' He sounded unalarmed and Faro said, 'How long has she to be missing before there is an official inquiry?'

Muir stared at him and sighed deeply. 'You're off again, Faro. You don't seem to understand that such matters are quite usual in rural communities like ours where young lasses like Bess, who spread themselves around, are concerned. They meet a chap, take an interest—perhaps a few shillings in it for them—and away they go.'

'You're implying that she's earning a living by prostitution.'

Muir chuckled. 'That's it, lad, you've got it right this time. She's the local whore, well known.'

'Sixteen's a bit early—'

'To be on the game, you mean. Never too early. Often with the approval of parents who have other bairns and are grateful for any coins that come their way. They see a pretty lass as a good earner.' He paused and added heavily, 'A fact of life, I'm afraid. And I'm sure you find the same thing in big cities like Edinburgh. Parents, most likely a mother, who turn a blind eye, happy to accept a pretty daughter's immoral earnings.'

Faro knew that was true. These were not only country matters. Every evening on his beat down Leith Walk or a glance into the closes of the old town could be guaranteed to reveal the sordid truth of Muir's statement.

'Set your mind at rest, Faro lad. The only way the police will be involved is if her anxious parents ask for a missing person inquiry and have evidence for their fears. And I have to tell you that from what I know of Bess's dad, that's not very likely. So don't you concern yourself, no need to lose any sleep over this one,' he ended sarcastically.

Faro thought of Bess's anguished mother, her tearful conversation. However Muir was right, it was no concern of his. He was helpless to do anything about Bess Tracy. His main concern was Erland and whether he was suffering from an aggressive form of food poisoning—or something much more sinister at the hands of or, more precisely, in the cocoa provided by Madeleine Smith alias Lena Hamilton.

CHAPTER SIXTEEN

On his way back to Red House, Faro had two significant encounters. As he walked along the main road past the alehouse, Mrs Tracy emerged from the local shop.

She looked weary and scared, her face still bearing bruises no doubt from recent altercations with her villainous husband. She would have walked straight past him, her head averted, but greeting her, he asked, 'Heard from your daughter yet?'

'Who wants to know?' she said, looking round apprehensively.

Faro wasn't sure how to respond to that question, especially when she demanded,

'What's my Bess to you?'

He decided to ignore that and asked, 'Are you worried about her? Does she often leave home for lengthy periods without telling you?'

'She never does. My Bess is a good lass. The lads are all fond of her, chase her and that sort of thing. It's not her fault that she's such a bonny lass. They're all taken with her, buzzing around like bees at a honey pot, they are.'

Faro persisted. 'Has she ever left home like this before?'

'Never. It's all her pa's fault.' Again that apprehensive look, over her shoulder as if avoiding a blow. 'He hits her and she won't stand for that sort of thing.'

Conscious that he was repeating the obvious question he had asked at their first meeting, he said, 'Has she a steady admirer?'

Mrs Tracy sighed. 'Oh yes, a nice chap this time, she said he was. A proper toff—' and looking up at him wistfully, 'a bit like yourself, sir, if I may be so bold as to remark on it.'

Faro bowed. A proper toff wasn't how he would describe himself. Perhaps his Orcadian accent, more in keeping with the Highlands than broad Scots, made him sound more refined than one of the local lads.

'Your daughter's new friend wasn't from these parts?'

'Oh no, sir, proper gentleman he is, like one of them artist fellows at Red House.'

Faro thought it extremely doubtful that

Topsy, Gabriel or Ned would be concealing Bess Tracy for the purpose of modelling as Mrs Tracy continued confidentially, 'I'm sick with worry, sir. Tells me everything she does. Every little thing she ever does, or anyone she meets. She loves her ma, does my Bess, and now I don't even know where she is and I'm feared that something awful has happened to her.'

Her eyes filled with tears and Faro said, 'Then you should ask Constable Muir to make some enquiries, officially.'

'No!' A shriek. 'Never that! Her pa would kill me if I ever let the peelers over the doorstep.'

Which sounded as if the brutal miller also had something to hide, Faro thought grimly as he realised that he was powerless to do anything regarding the missing girl. If her parents refused an official investigation, without any suspicious evidence, there the matter must lie.

And saying that he hoped she would soon return, with increasingly little confidence in that statement, he left her. Although Bess's morals might leave much to be desired, she was apparently a devoted daughter who confided in her mother. If this was true, then it was very irritating that she had not thought to reveal her new admirer's name.

A mysterious omission perhaps. But did she, or any child come to that, ever tell a parent every detail of such a relationship? From his own experience he thought not.

That fortuitous meeting with Mrs Tracy had given him food for considerable thought.

A toff for one thing ruled out a local lad. Had she met a stranger, a passing traveller at the local alehouse and gone off with him? Despite Muir's suggestions earlier, in the light of her mother's information, he thought that extremely doubtful and went on his way with an ominous feeling that there was something seriously amiss here, the same inescapable feeling he had had many times before in his brief career and these moments of intuition sadly were rarely proved wrong.

As he returned through the orchard, he had his second significant encounter of the day. The gardener who had been Erland's squire was now alone, pruning some late roses. He was obviously a cheery lad, whistling while he worked.

He heard Faro's approach, his feet rustling through the leaves and, turning, touched his forelock politely.

'That was a splendid job you and your fellow gardeners did at the banquet,' said Faro.

He asked his name: 'Dave, sir. We all enjoyed ourselves no end, sir. It was a rare treat, although all that dressing up seemed a bit daft—begging your pardon. All those masks never fooled anyone, even the temporary servants. Mr Morris and his friends are all so well known to everyone around

158

here.'

He grinned. 'The good thing was there was so much food left over that we were allowed to take it away with us. The lads who are married took it home and their families, especially the young 'uns, were right grateful. Never seen food the likes of that in their entire lives, bless 'em. Neither had many of the rest of us, come to that.'

He sighed. 'Food is simple and cheap and not always a lot of it. Mind you none of us working at the house can complain, Mr Morris is a good employer,' he added hastily. 'But banquets are special occasions.'

'I hope none of you had any of the shellfish.'

Dave shook his head. 'That was all gone. Some of us were sorry, we had never tasted much of that. But it was just as well from what we hear—nearly all of them down with food poisoning.'

He shook his head, whistled and said, 'I don't hold with the fruits of the sea, as they call them. My grandpa, who sailed with Admiral Nelson in the old days, said the sailors wouldn't touch them with a bargepole, never mind eat them. You see, it was well known that the shellfish fed on drowned bodies.'

It was a suspicion Faro had heard before in his Orkney days, heartily disregarded by most sensible folk.

'Do you board with the other gardeners?'

'No. I live in the village—my ma's a widow

159

now and I haven't got a wife yet,' he grinned and added with a sly look, 'Still hoping, of course. Aren't we all?'

Here was an opening not to be missed: 'Do you know Bess Tracy?' Faro asked.

The question must have been more abrupt than he intended as Dave laughed uncomfortably. 'The lass you were looking for. Oh aye, all the village lads know Bess.'

'She seems to have gone missing.'

'Oh, I wouldn't worry. She'll turn up again.'

'Let me know if she does. I'd like to meet her.'

'Oh, I will, sir. I will do that. You won't be disappointed.' And without any further explanation, a flicker of embarrassment changing the subject, Dave said, 'It was a good evening, last night.'

There was obviously nothing more forthcoming about Bess, doubtless a topic for lewd speculation with lads of his own age, but this 'queer cove' was older and in their words would approximate to 'a toff'.

'And you lads as squires made it an even more memorable one. A splendid occasion,' said Faro and on an impulse handed the lad a shilling. It was gratefully received and Faro had a sudden idea.

'I'd like to give something to the fellow who was my squire, but I didn't even know his name. He is one of the gardeners. Perhaps you can introduce me.'

Dave shook his head. 'Not one of our lads, one of the regulars, that is. He hadn't been told that daft thing, about not wearing a mask.'

'You mean he was a stranger?' said Faro eagerly.

'Not exactly. But kept himself to himself, so to speak.' He shrugged. 'We wondered why he was there. Guessed they probably needed extra help, and got some lads from the village or even Bexley. That would explain it, sir.'

Another thought struck Faro. 'Is Mrs Lunn's nephew one of your lads?'

Dave frowned. 'Don't know who you rightly mean, sir. Who might Mrs Lunn be?'

'She's the housekeeper at Brettle Lodge.'

A nod. 'Oh, is that her name? Heard of her, of course but can't say I know owt about a nephew.'

'She told me he is a gardener.'

'Is that so?' He shook his head. 'Could well be, sir. Some of the lads here have worked on the Brettle gardens.' He thought for a moment and added, 'Of course, gardeners come and go. It can be casual work depending on the season, although Mr Morris is most particular about who he takes on. Takes pride in being a good employer.'

Obviously a well-liked one as well, thought Faro, as he walked towards the house with yet another mystery to solve. Of course, Mrs Lunn might want to keep her nephew's presence quiet, especially if he wasn't her nephew at all and she was taking in a lodger and making a little extra cash—seasonally—when the owners were abroad.

A question remained unanswered and it troubled him. Was his squire, Mrs Lunn's nephew and the casual gardener mentioned by Dave, one and the same person?

* * *

Returning to the house, he went upstairs at once and knocked on the door of Erland's room. Lena and Poppy were there, sewing by the window, the floor glowing in pools of velvet.

'The doctor?' Faro asked.

'You've just missed him. He looked in, first thing,' said Lena. 'Said it was a definite case of food poisoning and that some people take it worse than others. He left some powder for Erland to be given every four hours.'

Poppy looked up from her sewing with a proud glance at her friend. 'He said Erland couldn't have a better nurse than Lena here, she seemed to know exactly what was required.'

He took consolation that Erland was not getting any worse and in fact was now claiming to be fit and regretting that the wedding had been cancelled. However, anyone taking note of his ashen countenance, and observing how weak and frail he looked as he tottered

162

downstairs to the dining room on Lena's arm, would have rightly decided that he was hardly a viable prospect as a bridegroom.

Lena was ever attentive to his every need, the dedicated nurse, her devotion a constant source of admiration. To all except Faro, who, despite the evidence of his eyes and Erland's apparent recovery, could not rid himself of a certain unease, a feeling that the story was not quite ended yet.

He didn't like the sound of those powders in her charge one bit. Of course as Madeleine Smith, she would know all about the right amount to administer . . .

With fatal results.

He was unprepared however for dramatic events taking place beyond the confines of Red House which were to divert his attention momentarily from his friend's well-being.

CHAPTER SEVENTEEN

As he left the dining room, a maid came over.

'You're wanted, Mr Faro.'

Following her out, he was taken aback to find Constable Muir waiting for him in the hall.

Realising some urgency concerning Macheath must have brought him there, Faro would have preferred some other place of assignation, especially as Morris and Rossetti, doubtless driven by curiosity at the maid's abrupt summons, had followed him into the hall.

A glance at their faces confirmed that the sight of a uniformed policeman on the premises was guaranteed to send a shiver of disquiet around the residents concerning their use of laudanum and other so-called pain-alleviating drugs, which in their cases were also used for the heightening of pleasurable feelings.

It might well also indicate what Erland knew and had promised to keep secret: that Jeremy Faro was here as more than just a visitor, not merely the country cousin from Orkney attending his wedding but also a policeman in search of a criminal.

Annoyed that he had not warned Muir more plainly, or the constable had conveniently forgotten, with a slight bow of acknowledgement Faro led him into the garden, hoping his confident smile at the wary expressions of Morris and Rossetti would make it clear that this was a social event and that he was not under arrest for some misdemeanour or other.

'We got some funny looks back there,' Muir said once out of earshot. 'Did they think I'd come to arrest you?' he added with a delighted chuckle.

'Probably looked like that,' said Faro grimly,

'especially as they don't know I'm a policeman.'

'Sorry about that, Faro. But I had to come—urgent like—even if it meant blowing your cover. There's been a burglary at the Brettles. Sir Philip returned from holiday—and guess what, the house had been broken into, valuable pictures, jewellery stolen. Sir Philip got me out of bed this morning—'

'Where was Mrs Lunn in all this?' Faro interrupted.

'That's it,' Muir said with a dramatic gesture. 'Vanished. Not a sign of her. Sir Philip found the back door wide open. I've had a quick look round the kitchen. There were no signs of a struggle. No bloodstains or anything like that,' he sounded regretful. 'Just a chair overturned. A bad business.' Muir shook his head.

'You think from this evidence that she has been abducted?'

'Or worse,' was the grim reply. 'And this isn't a local villain, I'm fairly sure of that, Faro.'

'What makes you so sure of that?'

'How would they get rid of stolen goods? Jewellery maybe, but what about those stolen paintings? Great big ones, they were.'

Faro thought of the railway link to London close at hand. Great big pictures in the goods van would doubtless be remembered by the guards. 'So what is your theory?'

Muir paused, rubbing his chin thoughtfully. 'If you want to know what I think—I think this has Macheath's signature written all over it. Yes, that's about it, your Macheath has returned to the scene and for more than a break-in to steal some food from the pantry this time.'

It didn't strike a note of probability for Faro, except that Macheath was primarily a jewel thief and a safe-breaker, as Muir went on, 'You'd better come back with me—if you haven't anything better to do, that is,' he ended sarcastically.

As Faro returned to the house to collect his jacket, the faces that greeted him were puzzled and apprehensive. He hadn't had time to think up a plausible explanation as to why he should be visited by the local police constable. And meeting Lena on the stairs, he wondered if the sight of a uniformed policeman brought melancholy thoughts of her own arrest three years ago.

Walking around the exterior of Brettle Manor offered no evidence of the burglary. Not that Faro expected any. Sir Philip had found the back door conveniently open and, following Muir into the kitchen, Faro examined the lock, which showed no sign of a forced entry.

There were two interesting omissions since his last visit.

The coat rack was now empty. Mrs Lunn's outdoor cape and the hooded cape which she alleged belonged to her lodger, a nephew who was also an occasional gardener at Red House, were both missing. He decided to keep this information to himself rather than set Muir off at a tangent concerning theories regarding Mr Morris's seasonal outdoor employees.

Opening the door leading to the housekeeper's parlour, immaculately tidy as befitted its owner, neat but dull with its table, chairs and sofa in front of a fireplace, Faro bent down to closely inspect the ashes before following Muir upstairs to her bedroom in the attic, where the contents of wardrobe and chest of drawers offered no clues to her disappearance.

'What do you think?' Muir asked the question again and apparently with no theories of his own eagerly awaited Faro's answer. Returning downstairs, he said, 'The ashes in the parlour fire are long since cold, so there is nothing to be learnt there but the fact that her bed was tidily made up does not suggest that Mrs Lunn was disturbed by the thief and dragged away in the middle of the night. Did you observe that there was no valise or evidence of a small trunk that a lady might carry while travelling?'

'So?' asked Muir with a puzzled frown.

Faro shook his head. 'From the evidence of our eyes, the suggestion I am obtaining so far is that Mrs Lunn left not too hastily or unwillingly.'

'It's fairly obvious then, isn't it,' asked Muir,

'that she's our accomplice who opened the back door and let the thief in?'

Faro nodded agreement. 'That also suggests that she knew his identity, and was perhaps prepared to leave but not in such a hurry that she hadn't time to leave her rooms tidy and make up her bed.'

He sighed. 'At my meetings with her, everything suggested that she was a conscientious housekeeper, although her honesty is now in doubt.'

'How do you make that out?' Muir asked.

'You have answered that. I also think it extremely unlikely that, although someone with whom she was acquainted might gain admittance to her kitchen on some pretext or other, she would certainly not admit a stranger into what she considered the sacred precincts of the rest of the house.'

He pointed to the green baize door, which had also been unbolted and unlocked from the kitchen. 'Where's the key, I wonder, which she wore so proudly on a chatelaine?'

Muir sighed, righted the fallen chair and sat down, his expression of relief proclaiming beyond any words that his feet troubled him sorely. 'Let's presume that the thief threatened her, made her hand over the keys, that sort of thing.'

'If that was the case, what happened to her after she opened the door—why didn't she raise the alarm? And, most important, where is she now?'

'You've got me there.' Muir frowned, looking longingly at his unlit pipe as if it might know the answer or more probably provide comfort and a constant source of inspiration in such matters. Reluctantly he returned it to his pocket, defeated by the sterile conditions of that almost immaculate kitchen, where only an overturned chair hinted at a struggle.

'Does her absence suggest anything to you at all?' Faro asked.

Muir thought for a moment. 'Perhaps he carried her off—forced her to go with him.'

Faro shook his head. 'Unlikely that he carried her off as well as the stolen paintings.' He could not visualise Macheath transporting her large person, fighting and struggling, in addition to the stolen paintings and added, 'Perhaps you observed what that unpaved drive, still muddy from the heavy rain, has left for us?'

Muir shook his head and Faro continued: 'There were two sets of large footprints, going towards the house and returning from it—'

'We've got it. The thief's!' exclaimed Muir.

'Alas no, they were yours. Have a look at your boots and compare them, if you don't believe me. But as we walked down that muddy drive I noted particularly that there was evidence of only one wheeled carriage, which had presumably brought the Brettles home.'

'That was very observant of you,' Muir

169

grinned. 'So our thief left no footprints and no evidence of wheeled transport.' Pausing he scratched his head. 'Any theories then how he left the premises?'

Faro shrugged. 'He could have avoided the muddy ground by keeping to the grass verge. But I also noticed that was fairly untrodden, difficult to achieve for a man carrying a heavy burden on wet grass.'

Muir shook his head. 'A puzzle right enough. How did he leave then?'

'There are lots of alternative exits in gardens this size, easy for a man to leap over a wall out of sight of the house.' Faro shook his head, looking towards the disputed cottage whose surly owner and his allegedly savage dog might have deterred a heavily burdened thief crossing his path. 'But my main concern is Mrs Lunn.'

'Has he murdered her, do you think, hidden the body somewhere?'

'If the thief was Macheath, it is out of character. He's a villain and a brilliant thief, whose success lies in moving very fast indeed. In the past he has taken care to avoid unnecessary complications by abducting or killing his victims. He has only one murder to date—that we know of—and that was an owner who arrived unexpectedly and challenged him with a pistol. Unfortunately he had not time to load it first.'

'But what about those valuable paintings?'

Muir put in.

That was a problem, but Faro put it aside for the moment, his mind racing ahead as Muir said, 'Sounds to me like he had an accomplice.'

'Doubtful, if we are looking for Macheath. He works alone.'

But even as he said the words, he realised that other possibility. Again he considered the possibility of Mrs Lunn's nephew, whose cape he had seen hanging behind the kitchen door, the cape that like Mrs Lunn's was also missing. A seasonal labourer according to Dave, not known to the rest of the team; had he also played another role as a squire at the masked ball?

Was he the clever thief they were searching for or . . .? And a sudden chill as he remembered another incident.

'I think I had an encounter with your local poacher the other morning.'

'How so?' asked Muir.

'I was having an early morning walk on the heath when someone took a pot shot at me.'

Muir's eyes widened. 'I doubt that. Probably old Boone out shooting rabbits. He's a sly old devil and he's been on my books for years now. Comes into the alehouse for a pint now and then. Brags to everyone that he's respectable now, given up the rabbit business. Old age and rheumatism has caught up with him instead of the law. That damned nuisance of a dog barking half the night was another cause for official complaints from his lordship. Even threatened to shoot the beast.' And with a shrug. 'Maybe he did.'

The old poacher dismissed, Faro's thoughts returned to the identity of the unseen rifleman on the heath. Was he also the mysterious gardener who had some connection with the housekeeper at Brettle Manor?

As he shared his theories as briefly as possible regarding Mrs Lunn's alleged nephew, Muir said triumphantly, 'Looks like, find Mrs Lunn and we've solved this case. You think there's a possibility that she was the thief's accomplice?' he added eagerly. Then with a vigorous shake of his head, 'No—I can't believe it. Not of Mrs Lunn. According to the missus, she's a regular churchgoer, Women's Guild and all that sort of thing. Not Mrs Lunn,' Muir repeated obstinately, 'She'd never steal anything.'

Faro had no such faith in human nature. If Mrs Lunn was not an accomplice, away to London with her fake nephew, her purpose served, the grim alternative remained that she had been disposed of permanently.

'We had better see Sir Philip,' said Muir. 'He'll be glad of an explanation.'

'And I should imagine he has already summoned the Metropolitan Police.'

Muir stopped in his tracks. 'No, Faro. There's another problem here. You see, it's very awkward, but Sir Philip doesn't want the big nobs brought in. Most essential that word doesn't spread around. He wants the whole thing to be solved locally.'

'For what reason?' Faro asked in surprise.

Muir shrugged. 'He didn't give me any reasons. Very firm about that.'

'Surely he wants his stolen goods returned and the thief apprehended.'

Before Muir could provide further enlightenment, footsteps in the hall announced the arrival of the owner of Brettle Manor.

CHAPTER EIGHTEEN

'Saw the pair of you prowling round the gardens. Well, any clues?'

While Muir shook his head, coughed apologetically and, stammering, strove in vain for a positive response, Faro took stock of Sir Philip Brettle. An impressive figure, well above average height and with the build of a wrestler. His still abundant hair was tinged with grey, the rather florid complexion and a watch chain stretched to its ultimate anchorage gave evidence of once handsome looks falling into the ruin of a well-seasoned dedication to good living, pointing in the direction of a steady indulgence in the regions of wines and spirits.

With an impatient gesture, Sir Philip turned his attention to Faro. Studying him carefully for a moment he asked Muir, 'Is this gentleman a detective by any chance?' He sounded eager.

Faro, conscious of Muir's rather resentful look, said. 'I am Constable Faro of the Edinburgh City Police, here on a special assignment in pursuit of a very clever jewel thief who has been robbing wealthy homes in Scotland—'

'So that is why you are not in uniform.' Sir Philip sighed, a disappointed man. 'You think that this might be your man's work?' he added hopefully.

'It may be so. And it happens, sir, I am the only one who has seen him face to face. In a very close encounter in Edinburgh I caught up with him. We grappled. I was unarmed, he knocked me down and escaped. We then learnt that he had been apprehended and was being held at the Abbey Wood police station. I was despatched immediately but by the time I came down, it was too late. No ordinary police cell, little better than a room with a barred window, could hold such a wily character—'

'An unfortunate circumstance, indeed,' Sir Philip interrupted, 'if you're sure this is your man.'

'I cannot be certain of that, sir, but the real reason I was asked to remain here was that Constable Muir received a report of a break-in at your home a few days ago.'

Sir Philip raised his eyebrows. He scowled at Muir. 'And why was I not informed of that, Constable?'

'I have all the details here, sir. The official report is at the police office,' and Muir produced a notebook from his pocket with an air of importance.

'Read that then!' said Sir Philip impatiently.

Muir read the rather dry account beginning with the date and time that the maid Bess Tracy had reported a break-in at Brettle Manor but that nothing had been stolen apart from food items from the pantry.

'The general assumption, sir, was that the burglar had been a vagrant in urgent need of sustenance.'

'Or a thief on the run,' was Sir Philip's acid comment. 'What about this Bess Tracy? What do you know about her?'

'Only that she was a maid employed to assist Mrs Lunn. Lives in the village.'

'Never heard of her.'

Faro thought that hardly surprising as Sir Philip added, pointing to Muir's report, 'No doubt she was sent by Mrs Lunn who would be very upset.'

Faro looked at Muir. They both knew that was not so, as Sir Philip added, 'Where is the girl now? Perhaps she could give us some explanation.'

Muir cleared his throat and said nervously,

'We don't exactly know her present whereabouts, sir.'

'Then I suggest you do something about that and find her sharpish,' was the irritable response. 'We are just wasting precious time, Constable, and the sooner we catch this thief the better our chance of recovering my lost property.'

Faro and Muir exchanged glances as Sir Philip continued, 'No doubt Mrs Lunn will be able to enlighten us as to exactly what happened. Where is she by the way? I expected to see her here, to have all in readiness for my return.'

Muir exchanged a glance with Faro. 'We don't rightly know, sir, she seems to have disappeared.'

'Disappeared?' Sir Philip thumped his fists together. 'Mrs Lunn and the maid—what the devil is going on here?' he demanded.

'Well, sir,' said Muir uncomfortably. 'We don't know exactly what happened. Mrs Lunn wasn't in the house when we arrived.'

'Evidently,' snapped Sir Philip. 'Do you think the thief has made off with her as well as her ladyship's jewellery and my two valuable and rather large Dutch paintings.' Without waiting for a reply, he asked Muir, 'Or have you a more plausible theory? Come with me.'

As they followed him upstairs, Faro decided there was a distinctly military bearing about Sir Philip and was not surprised to have this confirmed by his portrait in an officer's uniform on the landing.

He had fought for his Queen and country in India. But in that tour of the rest of the house, there were glass cases of medals, memorabilia and arms on display, none of which had been of any interest to the thief.

As for the house itself it was very handsome in a modern manner with none of the distinctive architecture of Red House. Although luxurious, most of the furniture was still in dust covers, suggesting that, unveiled, it would reveal a tendency to be ultra fashionable. And that meant, in Faro's eyes, to be as florid as its owner, with an indulgence in small tables cluttered with ornaments and bric-a-brac.

A tall man, he was already encountering difficulties in avoiding a plethora of large vases, undoubtedly Ming, priceless and large enough to hide a different set of thieves, those of the fabled Ali Baba.

Sir Philip threw open the door of Lady Brettle's elegant bedroom, its furniture shrouded, the postered bed neatly covered.

Faro turned to Sir Philip and asked: 'Was the room exactly like this when you discovered the missing jewellery, sir?'

'Exactly. Nothing had been disturbed. My attention was directed at once to the jewel drawer. It was open, its lock broken.'

Muir had taken out his notebook and

flourished it importantly, while Faro walked round the room. One thing was very evident despite the lack of clues. The thief knew exactly what he was looking for. Jewellery and a couple of valuable pictures. Was there more to it than that?

'Are you able to describe the jewels in more detail, sir?' Muir asked.

In reply Sir Philip considered the empty box for a moment then, closing it, he said firmly, 'Diamond and emerald earrings, a tiara. Pearls. Those are the valuable items.'

Sighing, he shook his head. 'I am afraid I was not familiar with the contents of her ladyship's jewel case. The usual things, rings, brooches, of little value. There was one difference, however.'

From the back of the drawer he drew out a small velvet-lined case.

'This contained the most valuable and irreplaceable item. The Emerald Star—a priceless antique.'

Muir whistled noiselessly and Faro, who had little interest in jewels, made a shrewd guess that the Emerald Star belonged to the India of long ago, long before the conquest of the Empire builders as personified by Her Majesty Queen Victoria.

He turned to Sir Philip. 'May I ask how it came into your possession, sir?'

Sir Philip gave him an angry frown. 'It is none of your business, Constable, but it came to us by honourable means. The colonel, my father-in-law, brought it back from India for his daughter's fourteenth birthday.'

His flushed countenance and sensitive reaction told Faro that he had come by the jewel in the time-honoured manner of conquerors. In other words, in that pattern repeated throughout history, with the listener left to fill in the grimmer details, by deposing or more likely murdering the Indian ruler and making off with all his valuables.

Faro regarded the empty case again. It spoke to him very clearly of Macheath. This solved one mystery, his sole reason for lingering in this area, for a very carefully planned theft. His next question was the obvious one in the circumstances.

'May I ask, sir, why this jewel was not kept in a locked safe?'

Sir Philip turned round. He bristled. 'Her ladyship did not think it necessary. She obstinately disregarded its value, a devoted only child it was to her only a precious reminder of her father. She refused to have it locked away and wished to have it by her at all times. Her lucky charm, she called it. A lucky charm!' he repeated scornfully and with a regretful sigh, added, 'She believed, quite wrongly as it happened, that the house was burglar-proof and that Mrs Lunn's presence was sufficient to fend off all thieves.'

His rather sarcastic tone suggested that he

did not share his wife's faith in Mrs Lunn and hinted at numerous arguments behind the bedroom's closed doors.

'That is all I can tell you,' he said, firmly closing the drawer. 'Are we finished now?'

'The stolen paintings? May we take a look?'

Sir Philip frowned. 'You may, of course. But there's only an empty space on the wall. That will tell you nothing.'

In Faro's experience empty spaces could give quite a lot of clues to a keen observer. He shrugged. 'Nevertheless—'

'Very well,' said Sir Philip. 'But this is a complete waste of time. Follow me.'

He led the way into the library and pointed to an empty space among several other less valuable paintings, mostly landscapes.

'May I ask the size of the two missing paintings?'

Sir Philip pointed. 'The two Van Meers fitted there—very neatly, with about a couple of inches to spare on either side. Constable Muir has their exact description,' he added wearily as Faro made a closer inspection of the wall and the polished floor.

Standing back, he regarded the space again. 'How long have the missing paintings been hanging here?'

'Since we moved in, six years ago.'

'This is their original position?'

Sir Philip frowned. 'They have never left it. In fact all the pictures were carefully hung. We

180

took great pride in such matters.'

Faro nodded. It was what he expected to hear. 'May I?' he asked before gently lifting the two neighbouring pictures firmly affixed by massive hooks to the wall.

'Do be careful, please!'

His inspection complete, Faro decided he had all he needed to know regarding the removal of the paintings. 'Were these pictures insured?'

'Naturally. All the items that were stolen were covered by insurance—but that is not what matters. These are irreplaceable items, some of sentimental value. Have you finished now?'

'Indeed yes. This is of course a preliminary inquiry, sir. The Metropolitan Police will doubtless send down detectives. The insurance agents will also need to make a detailed survey.'

Sir Philip looked momentarily surprised and, shaking his head, regarded Muir steadily. 'As I have already informed you, Constable, I do not wish the Metropolitan Police to be informed. This is to be regarded as a local crime only.'

Muir nodded and closing his notebook, he said anxiously, 'Several thousand pounds are involved, Sir Philip, as well as a rare and priceless jewel.'

It was a point Sir Philip declined to consider and waved a hand in a dismissive gesture. 'I

181

have my private reasons for this, Constable
Muir. Now if you will you kindly take another
look at the kitchen on your way out.' And to
Faro: 'No, not you. A private word, if you
please.' Muir frowned and darted a
reproachful glance at Faro for what was an
obvious ruse to be rid of him.

CHAPTER NINETEEN

Sir Philip closed the door behind Muir and
listened for a moment until he heard the
constable's retreating footsteps before turning
to Faro.

'I will be frank with you since I wish this
matter to be disposed of as quickly and as
efficiently as possible.' With a sigh he said
heavily, 'My reasons are that if the
Metropolitan Police are involved, unfortunately
they will have to know that I did not return
alone, leaving Lady Brettle shopping in
London—as I informed Constable Muir.'

Staring towards the window, he frowned. 'I
brought with me a young lady—a very close
friend,' he added hastily but not before Faro
had substituted 'latest mistress' for 'young
lady' as he continued, 'For obvious reasons it
would be wise to keep Lady Brettle in
ignorance of this, er, house guest, in her
absence. She might not understand—'

Faro decided that she might understand the situation all too well as Sir Philip concluded, 'At all costs she must not become involved.'

A not unreasonable request in such circumstances and Faro asked, 'May I enquire as to where I become involved in this matter, sir?'

Sir Philip winced and said, 'As you are a police constable from Edinburgh—a big city with which I have some acquaintance, you have doubtless considerably more experience than the worthy Constable Muir in such matters requiring utmost discretion.'

He hesitated a moment to see how Faro was taking this, before continuing, 'I mean, of course, in catching real criminals. From what I know from living in this peaceful law-abiding community for the last few years, all he has ever dealt with are a few poachers and those irritating gypsies, whose activities are mostly confined to selling clothes pegs and stealing clothes off washing lines.'

He paused regarding Faro's still face and went on with a despairing sigh. 'I am sure you can help him with his enquiries, especially as it occurs to me—as it has no doubt also to yourself—that our thief is the very same man you are down here to apprehend.'

Faro nodded. 'It seems so, sir.'

Sir Philip looked gratified, his smile indicating relief. 'Regarding the young lady. Most unfortunate, but I am making arrangements for her immediate return to London—before Lady Brettle returns.'

Faro decided that Sir Philip's anxiety and sense of urgency were justifiable as he went on, 'And you will keep this information—about the young lady, I mean—to yourself? As far as Constable Muir is concerned, I returned alone.'

'You can rely on my discretion, sir. One final question, regarding the character of your housekeeper Mrs Lunn—for it is not beyond possibility that the thief may have had an accomplice.'

Sir Philip's expression said that he was taken aback by such a statement. 'Why, Mrs Lunn is absolutely reliable, utterly trustworthy. Been with us for nearly thirty years, since our marriage. Came with the package, so to speak. My wife, I mean, of course.'

He shook his head, a look of panic as if the full realisation of the delicate situation in which he had found himself had now dawned completely. 'This is a dreadful business, dreadful.'

'Had Mrs Lunn any relatives?'

Sir Philip shook his head. 'None that I have ever heard of.'

Remembering the seasonal gardener from Red House who she claimed was her nephew, as Faro doubted that relationship and suspected that she made a little private profit from taking this occasional lodger while the owners were abroad, he kept silent as Sir Philip said, 'Lady Brettle might know of some, but Mrs Lunn never discussed any personal matters with me.'

'What about friends in the village?'

Again Sir Philip shook his head and Faro realised that he was no longer troubled about what might have had happened to his missing housekeeper. All his thoughts were engaged on his young mistress and the return of his lady wife as he coughed and added apologetically, 'There is a further complication. The, er, young lady has a husband, a Member of Parliament and any scandal would be a disaster, not only for the young lady herself but for her husband's career.'

Faro regarded him steadily and said, 'Lady Brettle will certainly want an explanation for her missing jewels, and the emerald, if they have not been recovered and replaced before her return in a few days. And that I fear is unlikely with the facts we have on hand,' he added.

'I have already thought of that,' Sir Philip replied sadly. 'Would you be willing to help in this matter, Faro? I have friends in Edinburgh, I am not without influence, and I shall ask for your stay to be extended in order that you may take charge of this inquiry. I feel there will be few difficulties since there is a clear indication that this is the work of the villain you were sent here to apprehend. What do you say to that?'

Faro agreed to this proposal which fitted his own reasons for wishing to remain at Red House until Erland recovered and hopefully finding some answer to the mysterious disappearance of Mrs Lunn as well as Bess Tracy, which no one but her mother seemed to take seriously.

He wondered how Noble would react to this request as he went in search of Muir waiting for him in the garden, easy to spot from the clouds of smoke arising beyond the ornamental hedge.

'Well, what was all that about?' the constable demanded suspiciously.

While Faro was framing a suitable reply, Muir grinned. 'You don't need to tell me, I can guess the reason. Our gentleman certainly did not return alone. I had a very embarrassing encounter with a veiled lady, young, elegant and I suspect very pretty, certainly not the horsey Lady Brettle glimpsed only from afar. She was taking a walk out here. I was smoking my pipe, and at the sight of my uniform, she took off at high speed. Obviously not the behaviour of an innocent guest. Most anxious not to be recognised. Guilty as hell.'

Faro gave a sigh of relief. 'Then you have guessed rightly what all that secrecy was about. Sir Philip has asked me to help you with your enquiries, which we are to keep to ourselves.'

'No Metropolitan Police to be involved?'

'Definitely not. And no mention of said young lady. As far as Lady Brettle is concerned, he returned alone and discovered the house had been broken into.'

'What about Mrs Lunn?' asked Muir.

'What indeed? I'd like to know the present whereabouts of that lady and exactly what role she played in the burglary.'

Muir rubbed his chin thoughtfully. 'An accomplice, eh?'

'The evidence certainly points in that direction. We must try and locate her first of all. What do you know of her background?'

'Only what I've told you already and that's precisely nothing.'

'Sir Philip did not know of any relatives either and we can hardly check references to her character thirty years after her arrival with Lady Brettle.'

Muir thought for a moment. 'What about this nephew she mentioned who worked at Red House sometimes? I know some of the lads—we meet in the alehouse for a pint and a hand of cards. I've never heard any of them claim to be related to Mrs Lunn.'

With a wry grin, he added, 'Not that such a relationship would make him popular since that highly respectable lady has a reputation for being a bit of a dragon. You could always ask the lads yourself,' Muir added.   -

'I will do so. Meanwhile, we might try the

village.'

'I think we'll find it's a waste of time. She kept herself very much to herself. We might try the vicar as she took part in some of the church activities, I gather.' He didn't sound hopeful.

The local church was first on their return route, the vicar walking slowly through the graveyard, staring at the tombstones thoughtfully, accompanied by a notebook and a heavy frown, indicating that he was seeking inspiration from the departed for his Sunday sermon.

Lost in a biblical world, he was startled at their sudden appearance. 'Mrs Lunn? Ah yes, the housekeeper from Brettle Manor, member of our guild. Regular churchgoer.' He sighed. 'And that is all I know about her. Family? None that I know of. Friends?' He shook his head, coughed gently. 'A very private person, I understand, with little interest beyond the confines of her employment at Brettle Manor.'

Faro guessed that in this close-knit, small community, snobbishly ruled, Mrs Lunn considered herself, by long association with one of the gentry, as a cut above the local residents.

They fared no better at the local shops where Muir was cordially greeted. 'Mrs Lunn? Can't help you there, Constable. Not a chatty lady, good day and prompt payment was all we ever got out of her.'

As they left, they were rewarded by the sight of the village hiring cab heading fast in the direction of the railway station. A glimpse of a veiled face at the window and Muir whistled.

'Sir Philip hasn't taken long to get rid of his house guest. That's the young lady I saw in the garden. Must be the shortest visit on record.'

As they headed towards Red House, Faro said, 'We could always try the alehouse.'

Again he got the reply Faro had come to expect. A shocked laugh from Muir. 'Not a chance. Things might be different in Edinburgh, but down here those that considered themselves ladies, like Mrs Lunn, would never enter an alehouse for the sake of their reputations, even if they were dying of thirst.'

* * *

Back at the office there was a telegraph from Noble. 'Keep searching. Find him.'

When Faro sent his telegraph in return, he decided that Noble must have second sight to have so shrewdly guessed that Macheath was involved. Later when he had time to sort out his thoughts and make some notes, he decided that Muir must have informed Noble in advance in order that Faro would be allowed to help with the investigation.

His main concern at the moment, however, was still Erland and his recovery as well as

189

seeing himself free of his suspicions regarding Lena alias Madeleine Smith.

In such circumstances he was almost grateful to whoever had broken into Brettle Manor and provided an investigation which would give him a chance to remain at Red House.

Hurrying towards the gates, his thoughts on questioning Dave's fellow gardeners regarding the identity of Mrs Lunn's nephew, he stepped aside smartly to let a carriage pass.

He was quite unprepared for the scene that met him as he entered the front door.

Morris, Rossetti and Poppy were motionless in the hall, their shocked faces, their sombre expressions told him what he least wanted to hear. It also told him the identity of the carriage he had met just leaving Red House.

Erland was dead.

'Just an hour ago. The doctor was too late, he's just left.' Poppy rushed forward and took his hand. 'He had seemed so well, getting better.' She shook her head as if to fend off the terrible memory. 'He just closed his eyes and—sighed.'

Faro heard a voice—Morris: 'It was totally unexpected. Totally—we couldn't believe it. That food poisoning—we've all recovered.' Bewildered he shook his head. 'No one dies from that. Feel terrible, but it doesn't kill you.'

But poisoned cocoa, thought Faro. That was a very different matter. That could—and did—kill.

CHAPTER TWENTY

Poppy was at his side. 'I'm so sorry. This must be awful for you.'

Not nearly as awful as for Erland, he thought grimly. 'Were you with him?' The question was so sharp that Poppy looked at him oddly for a moment.

She shook her head. 'No, just Lena. She told me—how it was,' she added awkwardly.

'And where is she now?' he demanded, aware that his cold tone showed a certain lack of feeling for the bereaved bride-to-be.

Gabriel and Morris retired into the drawing room and gently closed the door on his grief, interpreting his Calvinist reactions as too emotionally bound up to burst into tears as any of them would have considered quite the normal thing in such sad circumstances.

They were wrong. If they had known Jeremy Faro better, they would have realised it was far from the truth.

'Where is Lena?' he repeated.

Poppy regarded him tearfully. 'She went to her room.' Touching his arm, she whispered, 'She is distraught. Absolutely distraught, heartbroken. So unexpected. He seemed to be getting on so well, as you can imagine—'

What Faro was imagining was something quite different.

'We did all we could. Dr Innes came immediately, of course.' Poppy looked up into his face, clearly puzzled by his strange reactions. 'He has just left, minutes before you arrived.'

'Damn!' Faro made no apology. That must have been the doctor's carriage he met on the drive. If only he had known, been in time to stop his departure, confide his suspicions— Poppy looked increasingly bewildered when he asked, 'Did he sign the death certificate?'

'Of course.'

'Cause of death?'

'Heart failure, apparently.'

'Apparently!' Faro heard the anger, the suspicion in his voice as he turned abruptly from Poppy and headed towards the stairs. 'Where's Lena? Why isn't she here?'

'Jeremy!' she called. 'Please, I beg you, don't go to Lena. I realise you are upset, but she is the worst afflicted of us all. She did all she could for him.'

He ignored her and rushed upstairs. What he wanted wasn't consolation. Erland had been a friend who in truth had thought more of Faro throughout the years, remembering those early days of hero worship, than Faro had ever reciprocated. Guiltily looking down on the waxy face it seemed impossible that a few hours ago that same face had been laughing, teasing him.

Death had wiped out the adult years and

returned Erland once more to the Orkney schoolboy he had protected from his tormentors, leaving Faro ashamed that he had not done more to protect him as a grown man, his danger replaced by something much more acute. His unnecessary death at the hands of a woman who, regardless of a Not Proven verdict, he was certain had poisoned her former lover.

If only he had been present, seen Erland's end approaching. Now what he wanted was not grief and regret, it was justice and that he was determined to have. If he could prove that Lena/Madeleine had murdered this friend who had loved and trusted him, then he would get that justice and see her hang this time.

The tears were there waiting to be shed and, leaning down, he touched Erland's forehead with his lips, and said a last farewell.

Closing the door he walked across the landing and rapped on the door of Lena's room. There was no reply.

Cautiously he opened the door. She was sitting by the window, staring out, silent and unmoving. She turned to face him. There were no signs of recent weeping for a lost lover, no red-rimmed eyes as evidence of the distraught, bereaved woman Poppy had told him about, broken-hearted for the bridegroom who would never now lead her to the altar in the local church.

Looking closer, true she was pale, but that

was all. At Faro's entrance, she merely shrugged and turned her attention back to the window.

He could not just stand and say nothing. 'Poppy told me.'

She nodded almost absently, without turning to face him. 'Erland will be sorely missed—by all of us,' she added a moment later, like one already composing a conventional eulogy.

'Did he have anything to eat—this morning—for breakfast?'

Raising her head she stared at him, frowning, puzzled by such an ordinary everyday question, so out of context.

'No,' she said dully.

'Anything to drink?'

'Yes. A little drink of—of cocoa—he liked that best of all when he had little appetite.'

'Cocoa—your cocoa?' he said heavily.

She did not seem to notice and smiled. 'We seem to be the only ones who have a taste for it—too unsophisticated and unfashionable for the rest of the house.' And standing up, regarding his expression, she said, 'How about you—would you like some? So good for you—'

'No!' Faro almost shouted. 'I want nothing, nothing.' And bowing stiffly. 'I am sorry for your distress—I have also lost a friend.'

A twisted smile as she said softly, 'And I have lost a friend as well as a husband.'

He looked at her. There was no mention of love there. And she was such an actress, this

194

one. She sounded genuinely sad.

'Did you really love him so much?' As he said the words he had a rush of memory, a return to holding her in his arms at the masque, those passionate kisses he would never forget, believing she was Poppy and he had perhaps found at last the love he had searched for and never found. And the terrible realisation that she had tricked him, ready to betray her friend as well as her lover.

Clearly taken aback by such an odd question, she was regarding him open-mouthed, bewildered. A moment later she recovered. 'I was going to marry him, Jeremy,' she said and turned her back on him, returning to her appraisal of the garden in which Erland would walk no more.

*   *   *

Faro went downstairs, hoping to avoid Poppy as well as any of the artists with their condolences. Hurrying down the drive he knew exactly where he was going and exactly what he had in mind.

He would seek out the doctor and demand a post-mortem. It wasn't difficult to find him, a brass plate on the wall and the carriage Faro had seen leaving Red House.

A maid answered the door. 'Yes, Doctor is at home but—'

'This is very urgent, very urgent indeed.'

A look at his face convinced the maid and, a moment later, he was led into what was presumably Dr Innes's surgery.

'Do sit down. Now, what can I do for you, Mr—'

Faro introduced himself and said, 'You attended Mr Erland Flett, who died this morning. I am a resident at Red House—and I believe you signed the death certificate.'

A cautious look replaced the doctor's expression of polite concern.

'I want a post-mortem on Mr Flett.'

Dr Innes regarded him wide-eyed, obviously deciding that he was dealing with a lunatic. 'I assure you, Mr Faro, there is no need for that. I note from your accent that you are foreign to this part of the world. Maybe it is different in Scotland but we do not carry out post-mortems lightly, especially in a case of heart failure.' Pausing for breath, he added, 'I am curious. Why on earth should you want such a thing?'

'I believe that Mr Flett was poisoned.'

Dr Innes regarded him carefully. 'That is a very serious accusation, young man—have you grounds for such suspicions?'

Faro could hardly tell him that he believed the woman Erland was about to marry had poisoned her former lover as the doctor, without waiting for his reply, went on, 'I realise there was a recent outbreak of stomach upsets at Mr Morris's Red House. A great deal of

196

unnecessary alarm brought about by some seafood that was off at the banquet as well as considerable overindulgence—' About to add 'in wine and spirits', he shook his head adding, 'But hardly deliberate food poisoning. That is a very grave matter.'

'Precisely—which has taken Mr Flett to his grave.'

Dr Innes weighed Faro up cautiously before deciding that he was indeed dealing with a madman, his private opinion being that such people often graduated to Red House with its easy-going unconventional living arrangements.

'I am afraid I cannot—even if I believed what you say to be true—I cannot instigate such a procedure as a post-mortem. The police would need to be called in—and a coroner's inquest.'

'I am a policeman—here from Edinburgh in connection with a robbery.'

Dr Innes's eyes opened wide at that. He shook his head. False delusions, yes, even the law could be so afflicted. He had encountered many in his profession. He must be wary.

'I fear then that it is your natural training that inclines you towards treating any sudden death as suspicious.'

Before Faro could protest, he continued, 'I completely understand your feelings, young man. It can be very upsetting when it happens to a personal friend. You have my

197

commiserations, but I am afraid I cannot help you beyond offering some soothing medication to help you through this difficult time—'

'You can keep your medication, doctor. I don't want medicine, I want justice,' Faro said angrily.

Dr Innes stood up, his stern expression a clear indication that the consultation with this weird individual was at an end. 'I cannot help you,' he repeated. 'But I do most earnestly advise you to keep these suspicions to yourself and to try to banish from your memory what you have told me.'

Showing him out, the doctor said, 'I was not the regular doctor for the residents. It is possible that your friend consulted Dr Grant in Upton if he was in ill health. He might be able to advise you.'

As he closed the door Faro remembered that Dr Grant was the friend of George Wardle. If only he had not been absent on holiday and had received the message Faro left that evening, then perhaps Erland might still be alive.

CHAPTER TWENTY-ONE

Ill health had never troubled Faro. Feeling fit and well was something he took for granted, apart from occasional twinges of toothache

198

and extractions, which he regarded with the utmost dread. These were rare indeed, however, for he had inherited excellent teeth from his Orkney environment.

Now in a life free from any ills, quite suddenly on the day Erland died he was afflicted by a headache of unbearable magnitude, affecting his vision and bringing with it feelings of nausea and sickness. This unusual condition he was inclined to dismiss as emotional, caused by his friend's sudden death and his secret suspicions that he had been deliberately poisoned but as his symptoms showed signs of increasing, he felt sudden, justified alarm. Could he also be suffering from the effects of poison?

A little thought, however, told him that was not feasible, confirmed when he discovered that his fever was being shared by several of the folk in Red House. Morris, with his iron constitution and amazing digestive system, had been spared. His wife Janey was laid low, so too were Rossetti and Elizabeth Siddall.

Even Poppy was ill with what they realised was the dreaded influenza. It was already rife in the village and had most probably been introduced into Red House by some of the extra servants brought in to serve food for the masque.

Influenza was not something Faro had ever dealt with and he was determined to fight it off as he might have done with a simple cold in the head. His brave attempts were doomed to failure. Legs so weak he could hardly stand, his head thumping as if an army of drummers was within, he retired to his bed as the fever rode in and raged through his body. As the illness progressed, he lost all sense of time, so weak that even opening his eyes took considerable effort and trying to focus on objects was an agony which he soon abandoned.

So he accepted the inevitable, welcomed what might even be death for there was no power in him left to fight.

Occasionally he stirred to find a man, Dr Innes, taking his pulse in a very professional manner or recognised Morris with the chamber pot. Sometimes a swish of skirts and a dark female figure entered the dimly lit room, a nurse of some sort, moving about. A perfume he recognised too as she lifted his head for a cooling drink of water, forcing liquid into his dry burning lips, smoothing his pillows.

One day the clouds cleared a little and the perfumed presence became Lena.

He tried to sit up, to protest about what he knew not—a hundred muddled reasons, a sense of danger among them. Then with time lost, one day, it seemed, his mind suddenly cleared, the fever abated.

There was a man at her side. George Wardle. What was he doing here in Red House again? Their clothes were black, their faces sombre.

Wardle leant over, smiled and said: 'Good to see you awake, old chap. I shall have to take your excellent nurse away for a while.'

With an effort Faro turned his head and looked at Lena, as Wardle continued, 'She has looked after you very well and so has Topsy.' A look exchanged between the two. 'We have to leave you for a short while—Erland, you know—' he sighed, adding gently, 'the funeral.'

With considerable effort, Faro said, 'I must go with you.'

As he tried to sit up, Wardle attempted to push him back against the pillows.

'Let me go. I am coming with you,' Faro said angrily.

'That would not be very sensible.'

'Sensible or not, I intend to go. Now if you will excuse me, I have to get dressed.'

He swept aside their protests. Realising there was no way they could change his mind, Wardle said, 'Very well, we leave in half an hour,' to which Lena added, 'Get some warm water sent up, straight away, will you, George.'

Weak on his feet, Faro almost pushed them out of the room, closed the door and leant against it. Then, staggering about the room, washing in the basin the maid brought him, searching for clean linen, he regarded his unshaven face in the mirror. He had not time to shave. He must go as he was, if it killed him.

Slowly dressing, dragging on trousers and shirt, he was fumbling with a black cravat when

201

Morris appeared at the door

'Listen, old chap. We understand how you feel about this, but your going out so soon isn't advisable and poor Erland wouldn't want you to—'

What did Morris really know of him on such short acquaintance, or of Erland for that matter! He said shortly, 'I am going, that is all. Final.'

Morris looked at him, frowning, studied him silently, his grave expression saying quite clearly that he thought it might be final for Faro too.

He sighed. 'If you must, if I can't persuade you. Fortunately it's a fairly mild day,' and indicating the cloak he was carrying, 'This is fur lined. It will keep you warm at least. The wagonette will take you. Some of us can walk.'

Like someone awakening from a slow-moving nightmare, his legs heavy as lead, Faro followed him weakly downstairs. In the hall a gathering of solemn men, few of whom he recognised apart from the residents of Red House.

A few minutes later and they were following Erland's coffin into the cold dark church, listening to the droning voice of the vicar, the 23rd Psalm and a eulogy from Morris, beautifully delivered and extracted from one of his own poems that had been Erland's favourite.

Trying to listen intently, Faro found his

attention was diverted by the droning of a trapped insect on the stained-glass window (donated by Morris) and trying frantically to escape. All that life and energy in a tiny insect, he thought sadly, while Erland lay dead, awaiting burial in the cold earth.

He insisted on being one of the pall-bearers, carrying the coffin the short distance to the open grave, their solemn cortège accompanied by birdsong from the trees above their heads, trees changing colour, already shrouded in the rising mists of an autumn afternoon.

Faro found strange comfort from the ritual for the burial of the dead, its sad familiarity from long-ago funerals in Orkney and in Edinburgh, but none as poignant as this one. He had been too young to remember his father being laid in the ground, an event his mother had relived and retold over and over, his only memory her tears beneath her veil, his warm and loving mother, suddenly turned into a black-clad stranger with cold hands.

At last it was the moment of 'earth to earth', his right as Erland's friend and kin, Morris whispered. A handful of soil onto the coffin far below, then it was over. As they turned from the grave, Faro was aware of a figure almost hidden by the distant trees.

Too misty to see clearly a tall man, with a white beard, dark eyeglasses—and a white stick. A blind man, yet there was something about him that puzzled Faro, something oddly familiar. But even as he turned to look again, Morris was at his arm, ushering him into the wagonette.

'The man over there, the blind man, do you know him?'

Morris followed his gaze, shook his head. 'Never seen him before.'

'I wonder why he's watching us and didn't come forward.'

Morris smiled sadly. 'Probably just visiting a grave and stayed out of curiosity.' When they looked out again, he had disappeared.

So strange and Faro continued to be haunted by the vision of the blind man, certain he knew him but from where? Some friend of Erland's perhaps, but why that startling moment of awareness, out of context? He gave up the struggle, for the ceremony had, he knew, been too much for him, the shadows were closing in again, as weakness and mortal darkness threatened.

They got him out of the wagonette and into Red House, helped him upstairs. Someone took off his boots, helped him to undress and, grateful, he flopped back on to the soft white pillows, so exhausted by that short journey he felt as if he had been to the end of the world and back again.

He slept. Day became night, night became day, a moon arose and cast its silvered light across the floor and was replaced by golden sunlight.

At last a woman's hand, warm sweet liquid to his lips. He looked up into Lena's face.

'Drink this, it's warm and strong and it'll make you feel better.'

Hot sweet cocoa. He had no choice but to drink, too weak to utter words of protest or to thrust the cup away.

Hot sweet cocoa. But Erland had died.

Next morning (or was it?) he awoke, aroused by pangs of hunger and the drifting smell of toasted bread, bacon and coffee from downstairs. The door opened; Lena came in with a bowl of porridge.

He sat up slowly. 'I can feed myself.'

She watched him, not speaking.

'Where's Poppy?' he asked.

'She had the influenza too—a mild attack, thank goodness. She is recovering, rather weak too.' Removing the bowl. 'Drink this. You'll see her soon. She asks after you all the time. She'll be so glad to know you're getting better.'

He drank the coffee and, removing it, she said, 'The doctor will be looking in today sometime.'

'I want to see him.'

'And so you shall—he will be pleased that you have made such a good recovery. You were really very ill, you know.' She wagged a finger at him and smiled. 'You could have killed yourself, Jeremy, undone all our good work in nursing you, by going out the other day.' She did not mention 'funeral' but the

205

sadness in her eyes said it all.

'Well, I am fine now.'

'Don't be too sure—'

The door opened and admitted the doctor, a stranger who exchanged a few words with Lena. She came forward and said, 'This is Dr Grant.'

'Good morning, Mr Faro.'

Lena left them, closing the door as the doctor moved over to Faro's bed. 'How's the patient today? Dr Innes passed on your message, by the way,' he added while taking his pulse. 'This influenza outbreak has been quite devastating but you seem to have a splendid constitution. A few days and you should be fit as a fiddle again.' Suddenly serious, he added, 'I was sorry we could do nothing for your friend. Mr Morris tells me that while you were in a fever you were very concerned about him.'

Faro felt suddenly embarrassed. What had he said—what accusations had he made?

Dr Grant continued. 'You were very troubled; Dr Innes confirmed this too.' Head on side, he looked at Faro and said: 'I gather you imagined that Mr Flett had been poisoned.' Pausing, he awaited comment which did not come. 'I returned from holiday; got your message regarding Mr Flett and I came as soon as I could.'

Another pause, the doctor's turn for embarrassment. 'You were insisting that there should be a post-mortem on Mr Flett. Such imaginings are often part of a high fever. I expect you now realise that.'

Faro said slowly, 'Not at all. I am in my right mind now and I still believe he might have been poisoned.'

Dr Grant's eyebrows rose. 'I can assure you that food poisoning of the kind suffered by the folk here rarely produces fatalities.' He shook his head, attempted a soothing smile. 'I understand from Mr Morris that you had not been in touch with your friend for some time before you met here again quite recently. Is that so?'

Faro nodded. 'Not for years, I'm afraid.'

'Then you were also not aware of the state of his health.'

Faro looked at him as he went on, 'Mr Flett had a serious genetic heart condition. He could have died any time, without warning. He was aware of his condition but preferred to ignore it. Hadn't had an attack for several years and believed he was over the fits he had once suffered so frequently in childhood.'

And Faro's memory vividly returned to the 'doon-fallin' sickness' that had been the bane of Erland's young life in Orkney.

'A few weeks ago he fainted in the railway station at Upton. They brought him to my surgery and he told me his case history. He was in a panic, poor young man. Getting married and naturally, he wanted to know the truth. I did a few tests and advised him to tell his fiancée, Miss Hamilton. In all fairness, she must know—what to expect.

'I believe he did so and on his next visit, he told me that they had agreed to go ahead and get married. He still believed that, with due care, the medical diagnosis might be proved incorrect and that he would have a normal life span.'

He sighed sadly. 'As he left me, his last words were: "I'm not a religious man but if I were, I'd say 'We are all in God's hands'".'

CHAPTER TWENTY-TWO

So he had been wrong about Lena. Or had he? If as Dr Grant said, Erland had died of heart failure related to those boyhood fainting fits, Faro was still unable to rid himself completely of his lingering suspicions.

In part these were due to keen observations of Lena's behaviour which suggested that she was by no means as heartbroken as one would have expected at the suddenness of Erland's passing which, Faro coldly considered, also cleared the way for her to devote all her attentions to a new suitor, George Wardle.

And she made no delay, within days seeing their heads close together, deep in conversation, he wondered uncharitably if she was secretly relieved by not having the prospect of ridding herself of yet another lover.

That she was a wildly passionate woman, despite the serene and gentle appearance that had completely fooled a jury, had been confirmed for him on the night of the masque, a memory that refused to be banished from his nightmares and eagerly taunted him each time they were alone together. A glance exchanged and suddenly the distance between them seemed to diminish. A step across the room and the barrier would be down, their arms outstretched and he would hold her to his heart once again.

He shook off the image wondering how well Wardle knew her or knew of her past. He seemed a decent fellow, good-natured, kind and Morris was already proclaiming that he did not know how he had managed any of his business affairs before—fortune had indeed smiled on him when George had come into his life.

*　　*　　*

More or less restored to health and strength again, and enjoying the luxury of the house's portable hip-bath, Faro knew that he must establish contact with the police office.

Constable Muir greeted him warmly. His wife and daughter were just recovering from

the influenza which accounted for his concern.
'You were lucky to escape,' said Faro

Muir grinned. 'Wife calls it pickled in alcohol. Nothing like it for a barrier against infection.'

Faro wasn't so sure about that as Muir went on. 'Half the village were down with it.' And regarding Faro shrewdly, 'You got off lightly. I was sorry to hear about your friend though. Rotten luck.' And turning to some papers on the table. 'Sergeant Noble has been asking after you. Very concerned,' he said mockingly and handed him the telegraph.

'Tell him to get in touch, the minute he returns.'

Muir watched Faro's face as he read, with a sarcastic grin. 'Kind-hearted sort of chap, isn't he?'

Faro groaned. He was hardly yet in a fit state to go bounding after Macheath wherever he might be, presumably far from Brettle Manor.

Muir said, 'I still can't imagine how our burglar managed to transport those paintings without any kind of vehicle. There's a mystery for you to solve.'

Faro had his own ideas about that. Ideas he wasn't yet prepared to share with the constable.

'Lady Brettle is back, by the way, and is keen to meet you.'

'What about Mrs Lunn?'

'Oh, of course you wouldn't know. She was

with her ladyship. Apparently she'd been given permission by her to visit York, see some cousin or other and then join her mistress in London.' He laughed. 'Help her home on the train with the shopping, I expect.'

'Well, that is a surprise. Why on earth didn't she share this information with her husband?' asked Faro.

Muir sighed. 'That could have helped. There we all were thinking the burglar had done her in or some such nonsense.' He scratched his head. 'God's sake, do these well-off folk never talk to each other? Do they always have separate bedrooms and so on? Doesn't seem quite decent somehow. No wonder husbands go astray.'

Faro's thoughts however were on a more urgent matter. 'Have you considered that if Mrs Lunn was in London with her mistress, who opened the kitchen door and the one kept locked into the rest of the house?'

'Someone else had keys.' Muir frowned. 'The maid, that lass Bess Tracy.'

'Unlikely. By her own admission Mrs Lunn kept a watchful eye on Bess. Didn't trust anyone.'

Even as he said the words, he remembered Mrs Lunn's theory about duplicate keys. Her hints indicated Bess, but what about that nephew? He could have made a wax impression and, aware that Mrs Lunn was absent in London, seized the opportunity.

As he walked the short distance to Brettle Manor he decided that this offered some very interesting possibilities as well as links with the identity of the thief.

Find him and he might also find Macheath.

*   *   *

Mrs Lunn opened the door, the front door this time, but her greeting could hardly have been called genial as, without a word, she ushered him across the hall and into the library where Lady Brettle sat at a desk, head bent down, presumably catching up with her correspondence.

As the housekeeper left them, Faro wondered if she realised that she had been considered strongly as a possible accomplice of the burglar. Or even worse, that she had been murdered, her body hidden.

When Lady Brettle turned round to face him, Muir's description 'horsey' fitted remarkably well. A formidable lady indeed, large bosomed, her heavily corseted figure creaking at every movement, Faro found himself searching in vain for the remnants of a once lovely woman who had wooed and won Sir Philip.

Of course, had they been on more intimate terms, Sir Philip might have told him that it was never so. Like so many of his class, it had been an arranged marriage for money and

212

dynastic purposes. When it was doomed to be childless, his duty done, Brettle had lost all interest and a chain of young and pretty mistresses took over that function of his life.

Whatever Lady Brettle lacked in beauty she certainly made up for in intelligence as Faro soon found out, delicately rehearsing some probing questions, especially as Sir Philip had entered the room behind him. He now hovered, silent and listening, a hand resting on the back of his lady's chair. His darting looks at Faro could best be described as consumed with anxiety that he gave nothing away of their own previous interview.

And it was soon quite evident that this big, strong, aggressive ex-soldier was in awe of his wife and reminded Faro of a saying in the Edinburgh police that many a cock o'the walk in the force is just a poor feather duster at home.

As he asked for a description of the missing jewels, Lady Brettle turned to her husband. 'Don't hover, Philip. I can deal with this matter. I know exactly what my jewels looked like. I don't need you—go away, please, and do something useful.'

With a last despairing look at Faro, Sir Philip managed to leave the room with as much dignity as he could muster after his humiliation.

Watching the door close behind him, the formidable lady turned to Faro with a sigh. 'I understand that you are a policeman and,

213

fortunately for us, not from this area—or even this country.' A tight little smile. 'This makes what I have to tell you much easier. It must go no further and I must rely on your discretion.'

Already Sir Philip had asked for his discretion. What was this new addition to the domestic drama, he wondered, as Lady Brettle handed him a written list of jewels.

Reading it briefly, he asked, 'Are there any drawings of these items? They would be an enormous help in tracing them.'

Lady Brettle shook her head. 'Alas, they would be of no help whatever, neither would the list I have given you.' With a deep sigh, she said, 'In fact, it is my wish that this investigation is dropped immediately.'

'Do I understand that you do not wish to have your jewellery recovered?' Faro asked in amazement.

'That is so.'

'May I ask why?' He shook his head. 'This is a most unusual request.'

'It is indeed. To put it as simply as possible, if any of the items are recovered, it may well reveal the truth.'

'The truth?'

'Yes, Mr Faro. A very unpleasant truth. The real diamonds and rubies I sold long ago. My jewels are fakes. I had certain necessities, various debts of which my husband was unaware. I desperately wanted this house, he needed the money which I could not produce,

214

so I sold my jewellery.'

'Surely you could have told him. He would have understood your reasons for doing so.'

Lady Brettle froze at his words, all the warmth and confidentiality faded. 'I am not prepared to discuss our domestic situation with you, the whys and wherefores are none of your business. My only business with you, in fact, is to urge you to drop this investigation at once. I am not sure how far enquiries may have gone, but I understand it is only as far as the local police. On my instructions, Sir Philip was to await my return so that I might give a full description before taking the matter to a higher police authority.'

A very convenient arrangement, Faro thought, remembering his conversation that also made certain Sir Philip's young lady friend was not involved.

'You realise, my lady, that this matter is in the hands of Constable Muir, not with me. I have no influence over the decision of the local police.'

'Then you must think of something—some excuse. It is quite simple—that I had the jewels with me.'

'And the Emerald Star too.'

Her face changed. 'That too. Unfortunately it is the only item of value that was stolen.' She shrugged. 'Unique and quite priceless. Of sentimental value but alas there is nothing I can do to recover it without revealing my

215

unhappy situation regarding the fate of my jewels.'

The emerald was a definite clue to the identity of the thief. For if he was, as Faro suspected, Macheath, that alone would have fitted his partiality for safe-breaking and stealing valuable property from large houses. It also strongly suggested that he had never left the neighbourhood of Upton and disappeared to London, but had remained with the sole purpose of uplifting Lady Brettle's Emerald Star. He would doubtless be very disappointed to find that the rest of the items were fakes.

'There were other items stolen. Two Dutch paintings.'

She shrugged. 'That is entirely my husband's domain. Valuable, of course, so I believe, but not to my taste. Too dreary. I prefer Mr Millais myself.'

As did numerous other much humbler households the length and breadth of Britain, with reproductions hanging on cottage walls and in parlours of long streets in industrial towns.

'You must discuss this matter with Sir Philip. He is no doubt anxious to have his paintings recovered.'

Far from it, thought Faro, who had reached his own solution to that particular mystery and he felt a surge of excitement for his conversation with Lady Brettle had confirmed his suspicions and also provided a motive that, despite appearances, the Brettles were in desperate straits financially and Sir Philip at least had taken action to solve one aspect of the problem. It also accounted for the lack of servants apart from the loyal housekeeper and the occasional maid, Bess Tracy.

As he prepared to leave, Faro asked, 'What of Mrs Lunn?'

'Lunn was with me in London. She is in no way responsible for the break-in.'

Faro was not at all sure about that as he asked, 'Have you any theories, then, how Sir Philip found the kitchen door open with no sign of a forced entry?'

She shrugged. 'I can only guess that someone stole the keys,' she said vaguely. 'Had Lunn been here she would never have let them out of her possession for a moment.'

From what he knew already, that seemed a lame excuse but he said, 'I would appreciate a few words with Mrs Lunn, if you please.'

Lady Brettle stared at him, as if she would have liked to refuse his request before seizing the bell pull.

CHAPTER TWENTY-THREE

Mrs Lunn appeared and was informed that Mr Faro would like a few words. 'Nothing to worry about,' her ladyship added, observing the startled look on the housekeeper's face. 'Merely as a favour to us, to help clear up this inquiry.'

Mrs Lunn looked at him darkly as if she too would like to refuse this request for an interview. Then without another word she led the way into the kitchen.

Closing the door, she asked, 'Well, what is it you want to know this time?'

'This time I want to know how someone got access to your keys with such disastrous consequences.'

'How should I know that?' she bristled angrily.

'As I recall you carried them around your waist on a chatelaine.'

'Of course, and they seldom left my charge. Sometimes, when I was attending to other duties, I might have laid them aside for a few moments?' She thought for a moment, frowning. 'Anyone coming into the kitchen might have—'

'Anyone—such as?'

'Well, Bess Tracy came from time to time.'

'And you think she could have taken them.'

Mrs Lunn looked startled. 'You're a policeman, surely you realise that keys are copied all the time by unscrupulous servants,' she laughed mockingly. 'All that is needed is a lump of wax, heated at the stove over there.'

'And was the girl ever left alone to avail

218

herself of such an opportunity?'

'Sometimes—when I was needed in another part of the house.'

Faro's vague expression seemed to convince her, although he thought it extraordinary that she had such ready knowledge of how keys were copied.

'Are you aware that the girl is missing?'

She looked startled. 'What makes you think that?'

'She left home several days ago and has not returned.'

Mrs Lunn's eyebrows rose. 'Is that all? From what I gathered she had a dreadful life at home, and it wouldn't be the first time she had walked out to get away from that dreadful father of hers.' With a mocking laugh, she added, 'But missing? It's just an everyday occurrence with girls like Bess Tracy—I think you're making far too much of it. Making it sound far too sinister.' A pause and she added coldly, 'Is that all? I have duties to catch up with.'

Faro said, 'I regret having to detain you but there are a couple more items that you might be able to help me with. The two missing paintings from the library.'

She shrugged. 'Those dreary old things. I didn't even know that they were valuable although I dusted them regularly.'

'Did Sir Philip tell you of their value?'   ·

She quavered. 'No-o. But I kind of guessed—

219

why else would anyone steal them when they already had her ladyship's jewels?'

Why indeed, thought Faro. As he was leaving, he asked another question: 'Did your nephew also have access to the keys when you were presumably occupied in another part of the house?'

She stared at him. 'Nephew? what nephew? I have no nephew, who told you that—you must be dreaming.'

But his question had taken her by surprise. She was scared.

He went on, 'I mean your occasional lodger then, the gardener from Red House who you said came to stay with you while the Brettles were abroad.'

She banged a fist on the table and, red-faced, said angrily, 'I don't know what you are on about. I have no nephew and I don't know where you got the idea that I ever took in a lodger. The very idea! And if you intend rushing to her ladyship with such tales about me—she would never believe such a thing. You must be mad, Mr Faro, and I advise you not to spread such silly wicked rumours, ruining a lady's reputation like that.'

*   *   *

Mrs Lunn's statement had been absolutely accurate in one aspect, that of denying she had a nephew. The Honourable Paul, that young

220

man with the unlikely surname of Jacks, had claimed acquaintance having seen her in church. Her natural suspicions were soon put at rest by his charming manner and his flattery, the latter an experience new to her years and her long sojourn with sir and madam. While she was cutting flowers in the garden he had appeared. Watching her, he had volunteered the information that he was a gardener at Red House. Could she recommend suitable lodging?

Mrs Lunn was impressed by his educated accent, especially as he was such an ordinary-looking man, not at all that young or what she expected of the upper classes. His kind remarks were so reassuring, however, especially when he was so confidential with a sorrowful tale that he was only here because of a difference of opinion with his father, who was in the House of Lords no less, over an arranged marriage.

He must be younger than he looked, she decided, as with a gentle rather absent smile he continued that he had other plans, a sweetheart his lordship considered most inappropriate to his position in society. The only son and heir, he decided that his absence from the family home would give his otherwise devoted parent time to reflect.

A chance acquaintance had led him to Red House and as the gardens at the family castle were a showpiece, it seemed an appropriate refuge. Happy working with the lads there was one problem—the sleeping arrangements. He shuddered; he had never shared a bed with anyone as an only child—it was a new and unpleasant experience, especially as bathing facilities were not in evidence.

Mrs Lunn found herself in sympathy, even more so when he added that she was so like his aunt who had a title and both, he added, such gracious ladies.

As he stood up and thanked her for the delicious tea and bowed, afraid she might never see him again, she said hastily, 'I could give you a bed here—if you would not object to the kitchen sofa.' He eyed it and said it looked most comfortable, if she was quite sure it would not inconvenience her. Overwhelmed, he gave her a great hug. It was her birthday that week and not even Lady Brettle remembered after all these years. Her new friend brought flowers and a bottle of wine, which they shared. In the course of convivial conversation she showed him the rest of the house, giggling and stumbling rather a lot.

And that was that.

*　　　*　　　*

Faro left the Brettles. On his way to the police office, the rain began and Jim Boone's cottage would have made an easy and speedy access to the main road, he thought regretfully. Small

222

wonder that the Brettles had been so anxious to add it to their property . . .

The old man was visible in the porch and once again considering his friendly overtures at their first meeting Faro was tempted to walk over and have a cheery word in the hope that he might well have observed something significant regarding the Brettles' burglary.

However, remembrance of those threatening words regarding trespass, reinforced by the savage dog, at present invisible, was a sufficient deterrent against a second try.

As he walked down the drive his thoughts returned to the recent interview with Mrs Lunn, whose reactions to the missing Bess Tracy were similar to Constable Muir's. Why was it then he could not shake off the feeling that the girl's disappearance, taken so lightly because of her wild reputation, had sinister implications?

As for Mrs Lunn's downright lie, denying what she had told him regarding a nephew, the seasonal Morris gardener and her occasional lodger, Faro was certain that he held a clue to unravelling this particular mystery.

The steady downpour was a deterrent to visiting Constable Muir and he decided to return immediately to Red House.

Poppy and Lena were in the drawing room, sewing pieces of embroidery in cheerful colours at woeful variance with their black gowns and sad faces. All that was missing from

Lena were the widow's weeds to have added the ultimate expression of grief.

Faro could not escape meeting her while he remained under the same roof but realised that beyond the conventional remarks the suspicion that she had possibly poisoned Erland, despite the doctor's diagnosis, would not let him rest and would remain to torment him for the rest of his life.

He knew now that whatever happened he must leave this house, he no longer qualified for hospitality as Erland's friend and he should seek lodgings in the village. He had the words ready when the door opened and Morris came in with Rossetti.

'Leave us, old chap? You certainly cannot do that. You are still our most welcome guest and we insist that you make Red House your home until your business in this area is settled.' And turning to Rossetti, 'Isn't that so, Gabriel?'

Rossetti nodded eagerly. 'It most certainly is. Besides,' he added with a certain lack of tact, Faro thought, 'we have a painting to complete. I have just begun *The Rape of Lucrece* and those sketches of you, for which I am very grateful, have been of considerable help. But there is nothing like the real thing, and as Poppy is already modelling for another painting, I have decided to have Lena as Lucrece. She has a little more fire than our dear Poppy,' he added in a whisper, looking towards the two girls standing by the window, 'if you know what I mean.' He chuckled with a sly look. 'Besides it will be the perfect thing for taking her mind off poor Erland.'

From his short experience of modelling, Faro thought that standing still and silent for hours was hardly the best antidote for taking one's mind off anything as Rossetti said, 'Well, old chap, what do you think?'

Faro couldn't think of an answer except that the idea of posing as Sextus Tarquinius with Madeleine Smith as Lucrece was utterly horrifying.

However, the eruption into the room by Ned Burne-Jones with a domestic crisis about finances and the united cries of indignation that followed as they searched for an immediate solution gave Faro's future as a model a temporary respite.

*   *   *

As he left the house a second time for the police office, the telegraph to Sergeant Noble and his usual terse reply, suddenly the hopelessness of the situation overwhelmed him. Hearing the distant rattle of a train steaming north, seeing and smelling the smoke, he yearned again to be heading homewards to Edinburgh—to admit defeat, face Noble's anger and scorn, his colleagues' whispers as he returned again to his regular beat on Leith Walk, having thrown away this one chance of the first step on the ladder of his ambition.

Everything had progressed far beyond him, his futile search for Macheath and the extraordinary behaviour of the owners of Brettle Manor, their reluctance to have a robbery investigated because of the shaming secrets that would be revealed were outwith the limits of his experience so far with the Edinburgh City Police.

Erland's tragic death, the terrible suspicion he was totally unable to prove, that set the note of finality upon this assignment in Kent. To these were added his own surge of guilt, of being personally responsible because he had not warned Erland in time, and worst of all that he had never properly responded to the bond of friendship he owed his Orkney friend.

If he needed gratification for his visit to Red House, with reasonable grounds for suspicion that the theft of Lady Brettle's priceless emerald bore all Macheath's hallmarks, by a simple process of observation and deduction he had solved the mystery of the highly valued missing Dutch paintings.

A shrewd guess indicated that they would be found hidden somewhere in house or gardens after Sir Philip had used the excuse of the theft of his wife's jewellery to add them to a substantial claim for insurance, badly needed to ease his dire financial situation.

Faro felt certain that Mrs Lunn and Bess

Tracy were also involved, although he had yet to work out their exact roles and whether they were innocent victims or accomplices.

*   *   *

In the police office, Constable Muir had a visitor. Faro recognised Mrs Tracy, looking very excited despite her bruised face.

Muir grinned at her. 'This will relieve your mind, Faro. Bess is alive and well.'

Mrs Tracy held a note in a trembling hand. 'This is from Bess. It was pushed through the door this morning. I brought it straight here. It says,' pausing, she handed it to Faro, 'it says this is to let me know that she is well and happy and being well looked after and that we are not to worry about her. Isn't that right, Constable?' she asked Muir.

'Quite correct,' he replied and she said sadly, 'I never learnt to read and write—he—' the sudden quaver in her voice indicated the identity of her husband, 'he did all that sort of thing.'

'Has your husband seen this?' Faro asked.

She gave a slight scream. 'No! For God's sake, I daren't let him know I've heard from her—he never wants to see our lass again, has barred her from crossing the threshold. So I brought it straight along to the constable here.'

Faro turned the note over. There was no indication of when and where it had been written and Mrs Tracy frowned as Muir said to her, 'Well, you'll be happy now,' and to Faro, he grinned, 'No missing girl, case closed.'

Mrs Tracy however did not look happy. Glancing at the two men, she frowned and shook her head vigorously, pointing to the note. 'I hope you're right. That definitely isn't the way my Bess writes. I know I can't read but I've seen things she's written, like her school books about the house—'

Faro read, 'Dear Mum, this is just to let you know that I am well and happy and in a very comfortable lodging with my young man. I will write again soon.'

It was a perfectly ordinary note, the kind any girl who left home in a hurry after a quarrel would write to put her parents' minds at rest but Mrs Tracy was obstinately shaking her head. 'It just doesn't sound like her—those words—she didn't talk like that either. It's as if someone was telling her what to say.'

The note ended: 'I am delighted with my new life. I will come and see you soon. Your loving daughter Bess.'

Handing it back, Faro said, 'You will keep us in touch, when Bess arrives.'

He was sure that Mrs Tracy's instincts were those of a mother for a cherished daughter. As for himself, he too felt uncertain about this note and that there was something terribly wrong. It rang danger bells and he could not shake off the feeling that neither Mrs Tracy

nor anyone else would ever see Bess again.
Or even that she was still alive.

CHAPTER TWENTY-FOUR

Faro was wrong.

Bess Tracy was alive and the contents of the letter to her mother had been right.

She was indeed delighted with her new life. Her temporary home was much warmer and more comfortable than the horrible dark mill house where she had lived all her life, constantly hungry and cold and for ever evading her drunken father's blows.

Now although she was restricted to one room, it was full of small luxuries, a nice thick carpet on the floor for her bare feet to snuggle into, delicate china, handsome furniture with a big cosy bed and a deep armchair. Paintings on the walls too.

She was living like a lady for once. Looking around, she could hardly believe her good fortune. This was indeed the escape into another world she had always longed for and her only fear was that one morning she might awaken to find that it had all vanished, it was only a dream.

For these wonderful surroundings also included a wonderful lover, a lover unlike any she had ever known in her short adult life, who promised a future of so much more than this cosy attic room. A castle no less, once he had persuaded his father to allow their marriage.

Marriage to a rich lover, heir to a fortune and a title.

She closed her eyes ecstatically. She would be Lady Jacks . . . she frowned. She wondered about that name. Sometimes she even thought it wasn't his real name, far too common for a lord, but she did not really care too much. It wasn't important. Life was too good to ask questions and she had promised never to leave the house, but she loved her silken prison.

After all it was only for a short while, a week or two until things were settled with his silly old obstinate father who wanted him to marry a rich heiress who was fat and ugly.

Not like you, Bess, he had said to her. You're so lovely. No man could resist you.

Lovely words to think about when she was alone.

And that was most days, since he was off in the morning, sometimes going up to London to see lawyers, getting everything in order, he said vaguely. She never asked for details, content to accept legal matters that she could never hope to understand even if he had wished to explain them to her.

Her only worry, and that quite a small one, was her mother. She would be angry as well as anxious. Bess went on and on about it, so in the end he relented, but her writing was so atrocious, he made her write it several times. In the end he threw it away; her spelling was awful so he rewrote it for her.

She made him promise that he would take it to the mill personally and make sure that her Pa would not see it, that he would deliver it into her mother's hand.

That settled, for Bess there were no more worries.

The house's owner, an old gentleman and a long-time family friend she was told, had a kindly heart and had given the runaway lovers refuge. He had promised to look after her well when her love had to be absent. So far they had never been introduced and she rarely saw him or anyone else for that matter.

The attic which housed her lovely room had high windows and only by standing on a chair could she see down into the garden. Even then it was only trees that were visible growing close to the walls.

She could have been anywhere, in the middle of a forest for that matter, as there were no signs of the countryside beyond the band of trees, although she sometimes heard sounds of birds and animals, cows and sheep, a dog barking and she guessed they must not be far away from a main road with occasional sounds of horses and carriages and once during the night a train's whistle. He had brought her here after dark that night a week ago when he asked her to marry him and she accepted. He wanted their first night together to be in this honeymoon house, a secret from the rest of the world, he said. Just the two of them. So romantic.

He had met her with a hiring cab on the main road near the railway station and, once inside, they had travelled what seemed a long distance, although Bess could not be sure about how far or what lay beyond the windows, as she rather lost track of time. It all became rather hazy, lying in his arms, being hugged and kissed and responding so rapturously, only pausing to drink the brandy or some such fine spirit he had brought with him for the journey. She needed little persuasion to indulge rather recklessly although it made her head feel strange.

A toast to their future—another and another—just a sip—when all she had been used to with other men was a miserly glass or two of ale.

Such generosity painted a rosy picture of the future. Perhaps she even slept a little for when she opened her eyes, she was still in his arms, but they were climbing out of the gig.

It was completely dark, no moon or stars and he was whispering that she was to be carried like a bride over the threshold of their first home together.

After that first night of love she realised she had never experienced anything like this from the lads in the village who had been, what now seemed a long time ago, her initiation into womanhood. She thought of their fumbling hands, their gross thrustings, with a shudder. What bliss never to have to return to those experiences, which were considerable, as many of those village lads and an occasional visitor to the alehouse could testify.

After such a night Bess did not expect to awake alone. She expected him to be at her side, today and every day, with love unceasing, but he was up and about, dressed and ready to leave her. Kissing her fondly he said, no, he wasn't going to London, but smiling gently, did she not remember that he had humble employment as a gardener, for he had nothing from his father and he needed wages to pay for the rent of this love nest.

That surprised her, that they had to pay for this refuge, from the family friend, who must have a mean streak. However, he added quickly that he also needed money to keep them in food and new gowns and cloaks as befitted this new role in her life.

Gowns and cloaks immediately had her interest and he said that the old gentleman had a daughter who left home many years ago, but there was a wardrobe of her clothes still in the house. For these splendid gowns, cloaks and shoes he was negotiating on her behalf and very soon, as soon as he could afford to buy them, they would be hers. Meanwhile she must make do with the clothes she wore.

Bess did not mind. Having more than two gowns to her name suggested a new exciting experience and while she waited she was content with her new home by day and with a wonderful lover by night—although not quite as frequent as she had first hoped.

However, she was patient as ordered. There was always food and drink and such a future to dream about. She would have been worthless and ungrateful to feel for even one second, after that first glorious night of love, that there was something lacking in his attention. This she put down to the sorry business of persuading his father regarding their coming marriage and the need to earn wages as a humble gardener.

She hoped she might persuade him to come and meet her mother; she would love to have the opportunity to parade this lover before her hateful father before they left in triumph for that castle in Sussex.

As for Paul, Bess's lover, better known to Faro as Macheath, he was pleased and excited by his superb and unique plan. He had achieved his goal by stealing the Emerald Star. All that remained was the perfect exit, the perfect revenge in the death of Jeremy Faro.

Although appreciating the efforts of his secret accomplice, whose identity was beyond suspicion and worth every percentage of the shared profits of the many daring robberies he had engineered in Scotland, Macheath now urgently needed an accomplice here at hand to assist in the final downfall and death of Constable Jeremy Faro. Mrs Lunn had at once sprung to mind, but he did not altogether trust her, embedded with feelings of loyalty to her mistress. Information of when she would be absent with her mistress in London had been invaluable and sleeping on the kitchen sofa had provided access to the keys.

A lucky find was Dave, one of the young gardeners with anarchist tendencies, scorn and contempt for the upper classes. Courting one of the kitchen maids in Red House provided extra pairs of ears and eyes to keep him informed regarding Faro's movements. Neither of these young people had the least idea of what was involved. They enjoyed their roles, especially when they believed this chap Paul was a traitor to his class, and very open-handed with money.

Now everything was in place and Macheath relished the fact that he could have killed Faro almost any day, from their first encounter on the village street with himself in the role of the tetchy stubborn owner of the cottage on the Brettle estate (now the late Jim Boone residing permanently in a cupboard alongside his faithful dog). Once Faro was disposed of and before he quit this country for ever with a passage on an emigrant ship to America, perhaps he might rearrange that little scene so that the man and dog appeared to have died naturally in the hope that by the time someone found them all evidence of violence would have vanished with their decomposing corpses.

He laughed out loud remembering how disguise had been almost too easy as the smelly bewhiskered old man, to whom the villagers gave a wide berth. There had been so many opportunities for a fatal shot; that early morning on the heath would have done the trick. Another time near the orchard of Red House, he had waited, rifle in hand, but the door had opened, the womenfolk and their dogs rushed out. And at the masque, when he had stood behind Faro's chair as his squire, how easy to have poisoned his wine!

And in recent days seeing him leave Brettle Manor. One bullet could have rid him of his bitter enemy. He chuckled at those possibilities, but dismissed them hastily. Too risky and too easy. Besides, he was really enjoying the end of a game that had begun five years ago in Scotland. A game where he was the victor carrying off the spoils from raids on great houses, and the police had never tracked him down until one owner was accidentally killed and Constable Faro appeared on the scene and made his life so difficult. Now the score included murder, which was very trying.

What he really wanted in compensation was for Faro to suffer a long, lingering end, a death by hanging for a crime he did not commit. He wanted him to have that additional agony of mind as well as body.

As for Bess Tracy, he considered her coldly. He knew her kind: too ignorant, too lacking in imagination, food and drink and sex were the only ingredients she needed to keep her happy.

Not for very much longer. She had served her purpose. The trap was set, the girl the bait. He knew from previous encounters with Faro in Scotland that he would never rest until he had found the missing girl.

Jeremy Faro's doom was sealed.

CHAPTER TWENTY-FIVE

As Faro left Brettle Manor the first black clouds were riding steadily in from the horizon, the thunderheads already rising preparing for a violent storm as, with the first heavy drops of rain, he hurried into Red House.

There he beheld a scene in sympathy with the weather, alerted senses and suppressed excitement as Rossetti and Morris welcomed two new visitors, one a very thin, middle-aged, nervous-looking woman with a buxom cheery-faced, young companion.

Both ladies were attired in black, a fitting accompaniment to the mourning now adopted by the inhabitants of the house in respect for

Erland. Looking at Elizabeth Siddal's sorrowful countenance, and those other solemn faces, Lena's almost bright by comparison, Faro realised that Erland's death was an emotional situation they were well able to deal with.

He had already observed the mysterious agony of love with its drooping heavy-lidded frustration, the unspeakable sadness of loss in which they had a merciless indulgence. The endless sorrowful saga, the cruel tragedies of the medieval knights and ladies with their doomed love, provided the background of their everyday lives. It was life and breath, the integral ingredient, of the Pre-Raphaelite movement, a theatrical sense of drama which they exploited to the full and enjoyed considerably more than any mundane straightforward relationship.

As Faro was introduced to Madame Pireau and her daughter Euphemia, Morris whispered, 'We weren't expecting you, old chap. These ladies are our invited guests, come down specially. We are to hold a seance.'

The maids were drawing the curtains, an unnecessary precaution since the room was threatened by the darkness of the approaching storm, the rumble of distant thunder.

'A seance?' Faro had never associated the practical William Morris with the new fad of spiritualism which had its origins in America but had taken Britain by storm a few years ago in 1852. Getting in touch with the dear departed was sweeping the country, in no small measure thanks to the enthusiasm of novelist Charles Dickens who had achieved phenomenal success with *A Christmas Carol*, and Her Gracious Majesty Queen Victoria would be persuaded to believe that she could get in contact with her beloved Albert after his death in 1861.

Inevitably the spiritualist movement had its trail of charlatans as well as true believers. Rossetti perhaps interpreting Faro's astonished and doubtful expression said hastily, 'Madame Pireau is a medium, she has proved many times that the spirits of those we loved who are on the other side now keep constant watch over us. Their help is invaluable. They can not only advise but also warn us. They are all around us,' he made a dramatic gesture, 'everywhere! In constant attendance, just waiting to be summoned.'

Faro nodded vaguely, his cynical thoughts that the spirits that inhabited Red House most often came out of a bottle, not from hands eager to be linked over the small round table that was being carried into the room.

Rossetti looked towards Lena, as she talked politely to the new arrivals. 'This visit was arranged several weeks ago. Madame has just returned from a triumphant American tour. Topsy thought we ought to cancel it—Erland, you know—' he added in a whisper, 'but Janey and Elizabeth persuaded him that this visit was well timed indeed, the spirits themselves could not have done better.'

Looking towards Lena, as she talked politely to the two guests, he nodded sadly. 'And I agreed. In fact, we all decided that it might help dear Lena in her sad loss, cheer her up to know that she might be put in touch with Erland again.'

Faro doubted that, as Lena's calm untroubled expression, gently smiling at Euphemia Pireau, showed less grief at that moment than any of Erland's friends who had followed his coffin to the grave.

The medium's daughter was throwing over the table a circular black cloth edged with large white letters of the alphabet. From her basket she produced a large glass tumbler, which she set in the centre.

Rossetti pointed to it. 'Madame has just told us, she was advised by her guide, who had a severe cold and had lost her voice, to use this method instead. We all place a finger on the glass and it moves to spell out words. She has found it extremely useful to help reluctant or shy spirits to declare themselves.'

He regarded Faro anxiously. 'We would be delighted if you would join us. Perhaps you have a loved one . . .'

The only loved one Faro would have liked to have heard from was his policeman father, Constable Magnus Faro, whose death his mother stoutly maintained was murder, but he doubted the solution of that particular mystery was within the powers of any spirit guide.

With little desire to take part in this experience, he realised it would be churlish to refuse and he decided to sit down at the table with the others, somewhat unwillingly perhaps, but nevertheless with a sense of curiosity. Although he scorned such procedures, the instincts of a detective in him hinted that there was trickery involved, which he would observe with a very watchful eye, eager to know how the two women made it work.

As if his thoughts were overheard, Madame said, 'I must warn you not to expect too much. Sometimes, although we all have our fingers on the glass, it either refuses to move or else travels round the table at high speed, spelling out gibberish nonsense. We must prepare ourselves for disappointment; sometimes the spirits are not in the right frame of mind and my guide, a small girl, can be disagreeable and sullen.'

She paused, and added darkly, 'Sometimes we have to realise that elementals have invaded and are in our midst. Elementals are bad spirits, and it is advisable then to close down our experiments immediately.'

Listening, Faro decided that this was all nonsense, but at least entertaining. As for the presence of bad spirits, he hoped he would be able to keep a straight face.

Seated around the table were Madame and her daughter, Rossetti, Elizabeth, Morris, Janey, with himself between Poppy and Lena.

'We will begin with a prayer for protection,' said Madame. 'Our Father, which art in heaven—'

The Lord's Prayer, inappropriate company for Morris and Rossetti, would at least take care of the elementals, Faro thought, glancing around at the bowed heads, eyes firmly lowered.

'Amen. Amen.'

Madame lifted her head. 'Our hands linked, we will begin in the usual way.' A pause. 'Is there anyone there? One rap for yes, two for no.'

There was no response. She tried again, then a third time. By then Faro's limited patience was at an end.

Madame sighed. 'We will now proceed with our alternative. Fingertips on the glass if you please, and I beg you let them remain stationary. The spirits will do the rest.' A pause. 'Is there anyone there?'

The table rocked gently, a shudder then stillness.

'Have you a message for anyone here?'

The silence was shattered by a loud clap of thunder as rain beat on the windows. Through a gap in the curtains, lightning flashed.

Faro-began counting as he had been taught long ago, how many miles before they were in the eye of the storm.

As Madame repeated her question, another wait was involved and Faro sensed a flutter of impatience, a suppressed sigh round the table.

Then the glass moved, began to search out letters.   F—A—R—D—E—A—T—H.   It stopped. Looks were exchanged, Madame smiled indulgently. 'Oh, the spirits are up to their tricks again, telling us what we know already, that we must all leave this earth. Hush—'

The glass was moving again. 'What is your message?'

'E M I L . . . E M I L . . .'

The glass stopped. Madame said: 'Sometimes they can't spell very well. Do we have an Emily here? No. Continue, spirit, tell us who you have a message for?'

'M I M I—M Y—M I M I . . .'

Another smile from Madame, a look around the table. 'Do we have a Mimi?' Looks were exchanged, heads shaken.

'Dear me. Very well. What have you to tell your Mimi, spirit?'

'W h y—d i d—y o u—'

Silence again. Madame shook her head. 'Continue, spirit—'

'M i m i—why did you ki—k—k—'

Before the word could continue, at his side, Lena's finger left the glass. She stood up sharply. 'I'm unwell. The thunder you know— affects my head. Please excuse me.'

Hurriedly pushing back the chair, she fled from the room.

Looks of consternation were exchanged. At Faro's side, Poppy whispered, 'Poor Lena, I must go to her. She suffers from frightful headaches.' And to Madame, 'Miss Hamilton has been very recently bereaved. The day before her wedding,' she ended on a sob and a reproachful look towards Morris and Gabriel, indicating that this was all their fault for upsetting Lena.

Rossetti had left the table, and opened the curtains. 'My apologies, Madame, perhaps we can try later. I am sorry about this. I thought it would cheer Miss Hamilton, that her dear bridegroom might get in touch with her.'

Faro declined the tea and sandwiches that the maids had been summoned to bring. Madame Pireau was also upset and her daughter was administering the smelling salts. Doubtless she was rather angry since her much vaunted attempts to raise the spirits of the dead had failed so utterly.

He heard her say to Janey Morris, who had taken her hand, 'If only our spirit guide had been permitted to finish that message. It is extremely dangerous to be interrupted like that. And now we will never know how important the message was.'

Faro slowly climbed the stairs to his room. The storm was wild now, as if indeed the spirits were out in an army trying to invade

Red House, hurling themselves against the windows.

In his room he closed the door. For an unbeliever like himself, it had been an interesting experience and he had interpreted much which was lost on the others. 'Far—' that could well have been 'Faro—death.' A kindly warning he did not care to consider too deeply, as danger and death were the constant hazards of his existence.

But only he knew the truth of that abortive seance. There was no mysterious Emily; the glass had been trying to spell out Emile, whose pet name for Madeleine had been Mimi.

'Why did you ki—' Was the word Lena had interrupted by her flight 'kill' and was the tormented spirit of Emile d'Angelier wishing to know why his Mimi had killed him?

His normally acute powers of observation and deduction, about the futile quest of being sent down to Kent to track down Macheath, had been clouded over by the shock of meeting Madeleine Smith as Lena Hamilton and his deep concern for Erland's coming marriage to her.

Erland's death had been the final straw, and the fact that the doctor refused to countenance that he had perhaps been poisoned stoutly maintaining that, as he had suffered heart failure, there would certainly be no reason for a post-mortem.

Then something happened that cast all

thoughts of Madeleine Smith aside, enlightenment that changed the whole complex of the missing Macheath.

He knew that the answer to the one vital piece of the puzzle had been with him every day.

From the beginning—his first day at Red House—staring him in the face although he had failed to recognise it.

CHAPTER TWENTY SIX

Abandoning the seance, he had returned to his bedroom and was considering the next entry for his logbook. Because of his preoccupation with Madeleine and Erland this usually invaluable device had failed to provide him with the necessary clues.

Now Erland was dead and all that remained was that he track down Macheath and solve what had happened to Bess Tracy and return as soon as possible to Edinburgh where he might honourably resume his association with Lizzie, although he had to admit, however reluctantly, that the exotic womenfolk at Red House, particularly the model Poppy, had cast doubts on his feelings for her.

As for the events at Brettle Manor, they rested firmly in the province of Constable Muir, since the Brettles, both for their own secret reasons, declined the assistance of the Metropolitan Police. How the constable would cope with this problem was not his concern, although the possible outcome intrigued him.

All these events were outlined in his logbook, including the abortive interviews with the Brettles and with Mrs Lunn. He hoped that entering the details in his logbook would clear his mind and direct his thoughts into more positive channels.

'If in doubt write it down, every fact that you know and what is missing is invariably where the solution lies.'

Such had been McFie's words when he recommended this device at their first meeting and Faro's log conscientiously dated day by day the chronicle of his futile search for Macheath, the telegraphs to Edinburgh and Noble's terse replies, his interviews with Mrs Lunn.

Faro's certainty that Macheath had stolen the Emerald Star now justified what had seemed a futile pursuit as well as Noble's faith in his ability to track down this particularly elusive criminal.

'Remain in Upton.' But as he wrote the words, Faro asked himself: Had Macheath, as Mrs Lunn's lodger, found the perfect opportunity to make wax impressions of the keys? At last the right moment had arrived when she had departed to London and the house was empty.

Perhaps Mrs Lunn had her own suspicions and because this new acquaintance might implicate her with the theft, had denied all knowledge of the occasional seasonal gardener whom she had previously claimed to Faro was her nephew.

Faro shook his head. From information thus far he realised one important fact that he had overlooked. To remain in the district and keep an eye on Brettle Manor, Macheath must have a base somewhere near at hand. But where?

Laying aside the logbook, he realised that he must retrace his steps. As he walked through the orchard taking the short cut to Brettle Manor, the gardeners were busy with their early autumn activities and acknowledged him with their usual polite greetings.

Deep in thought at last he walked down the drive and stood by the kitchen door, looking towards the cottage so hotly disputed and he realised there was in fact only one place for Macheath's vigil.

Faro knew then that he had guessed part of the truth, but was the old man sitting in the porch his accomplice? Faro thought not, considering what he knew of the recluse via Muir and the alehouse gossip. Boone had been curious enough about Faro as a stranger to the district and apparently eager to be friendly at their first meeting in the village. Why then had he turned so hostile when Faro approached him on a visit to Brettle Manor.

Then there was the dog, whose barking had kept intruders at bay and Sir Philip off his sleep. The dog no longer barked at his distant approach or was even visible as a warning presence. He thought it unlikely that Sir Philip had shot the animal as he had threatened. However, bearing in mind that Macheath was a master of disguise, that present scene outside the cottage had suddenly taken on a more chilling and sinister interpretation. Was Boone still alive?

Excited by what he had revealed, all that now remained was to confront Macheath. How he was to accomplish this, he had as yet no clear idea. There were certain obvious disadvantages, being unarmed when faced with a killer ready to fight for his life.

As for Bess, where did she fit into this puzzle? Indeed, was she still alive?

Even as these thoughts engaged Faro's powers of concentration, he need not have been too concerned, for the idea of confrontation was also at that moment engaging the mind of Macheath with Faro as his objective.

In one thing Macheath was wrong about Bess. The added ingredients he had overlooked—so common in most women— were curiosity and boredom. She soon got bored if he was not around to make love to her all day. It was an accident however that triggered off the baited trap prematurely before he was ready or had his target Jeremy Faro firmly in place.

Bess had only one gown, the one she had been wearing for several days while he was making provision for that mythical wardrobe. Unfortunately Bess's monthly bleeding began suddenly and heavily and her pale-yellow dress was stained. Standing in her shift, she realised that this was a valid reason and opportunity to search around for that promised wardrobe of handsome gowns and cloaks. It was doubtful that the house's owner, the family friend, would remember exactly what his daughter had worn and Bess felt sure that one gown would never be missed.

She often thought about the old gentleman who lived on the ground floor and spent so much time smoking in the garden. He also provided her meals. They were not always punctual. Sometimes she was quite hungry and, without a clock, nothing to guide her beyond hunger pangs, daylight and darkness. She had learnt to content herself with the generous supply of sweetmeats her lover had provided and await the arrival of a tray along with water for her ablutions, which were placed at the bottom of the flight of stairs leading to her attic room, cut off from the rest of the house by a locked door.

Denied any communication with the bearer, who as her lover told her was old, her curiosity was aroused by his footsteps, which sounded light and quick, and she would have welcomed a word with him. She therefore determined on a closer acquaintance.

Once hearing his approach, she called out a greeting. He turned and scuttled away leaving her with only a glimpse of white hair. At the sound of a key turned in the lock, for the first time she had to acknowledge that she was virtually a prisoner in this house, albeit a happy one.

As for the house's owner, men, as she knew from her already vast experience, were odd creatures. Some were bold and some were painfully shy and afraid of women. The old gentleman obviously belonged to the latter but as her lover's family friend who had offered them this safe refuge, she felt a little hurt and neglected.

But she was happier now than she had ever been in her short life, ashamed to admit boredom with the silence of her attic room, invaded only by distant sounds of carriages from a main road beyond the wooded garden. Once she heard a dog barking—she wished she could see it, she liked dogs.

With the gown waiting to be washed, this was a good excuse to go in search of some suitable garment. Her lover might return at any moment and she did not want to be found by him in a ragged shift that had once belonged to her mother.

As she slipped downstairs, the attic door was

not the problem she had expected. The lock was old and rusted, a determined push and it yielded to her shoulder. As it sprang open she hoped the noise had not been heard and looked out cautiously.

There was no sound of movement in the house, but she must hurry. Soon it would be dark. From the landing, looking out of the window, she realised that she knew exactly where she was now. Although the treetop view from the attic had concealed the contours of the adjacent countryside, the area she now looked on was familiar and indeed not far distant from her home.

She did not linger. Caution and speed were essential. Far below on the porch, she caught a glimpse of the old gentleman with his clay pipe. She certainly did not want to attract his attention and have to explain what she was doing downstairs in her shift.

She looked along the dark landing. Two doors, presumably bedrooms. Opening the nearest, it was apparently used for storage, the entire floor area heaped with silver and ornaments of all shapes and sizes, doubtless the old gentleman's hoard of a lifetime's possessions.

No wardrobe however was visible.

The second bedroom was completely empty, the old gentleman must now sleep downstairs, although remembering those light footsteps he had not yet reached the stage of finding stairs a trial.

She sniffed the air. Although the room was empty, there was a distinctly unpleasant smell, a slightly sweet, animal smell. Not the sort of room she'd want to linger in, with only a wall cupboard alongside the old fireplace. This cupboard she decided must be the wardrobe where the gowns were stored.

Excited now, she went to open the door, expecting a flood of bright colour, frail perfume.

Instead the unpleasant smell was decidedly stronger, so strong she held her breath. It was too dark to see the interior clearly but there was the first disappointment.

Not a single gown, just a tumbled heap of clothes on the floor and a mass of shabby fur. The smell was awful, she leant forward and touched the bundle of clothes. A face appeared, a gnarled hand.

She screamed. An old man's face, bewhiskered, pale, the mouth open as if in a noiseless cry. And at his side, the matted fur took shape now in the body of a mongrel dog.

Both were dead! And neither by natural causes. She knew in that instant that they had been murdered.

Trembling she stood up and, sobbing, ran from the room. She had to escape from this terrible scene, this lovely home, this lovers' refuge now tainted with such horror.

At the bottom of the stairs, clutching the

banister, she stopped in her flight. Terrified, confused by this discovery, one thought penetrated.

Who did the bodies belong to? How long had they lain hidden in that unlocked room? About to open the front door, some instinct—a sense of caution—made her hesitate.

If the man and his dog were dead—who then was the old gentleman she had seen out there, smoking his pipe in the garden?

All thoughts of a lovely wardrobe vanished, taking her prudent lover with it as a dream of love exploded into a terrible reality. There was a cloak hanging behind the front door.

She had to escape. She pulled it on as she opened the front door and ran out, just as the old man with white hair was crossing the garden.

She ran and ran towards the village. She had to find help. Aware that time was not on her side, and of her terrible danger, she did not run for home. It was too far away, he would catch up with her.

She panicked. Red House was nearer.

She knew some of the gardeners intimately. They would know what to do. They would help her.

CHAPTER TWENTY-SEVEN

Macheath saw her leave the house, running, obviously something amiss as she would not willingly disobey him.

It took him just seconds to whip off the old hat and beard and throw on the gardener's hooded cape. He could move like lightning and had no difficulty catching up with her just as she reached the gate leading to Red House.

As Paul Jacks he turned on all his charm and concern. She clung to him, sobbing out a terrified story about a dead man and a dog hidden in a cupboard. A totally unexpected blow to his plan for her.

Expecting to be chided for running away, for disobeying his orders, Bess was consoled that he wasn't angry, said this was a serious matter indeed. But there was one man who could help them.

This man was a policeman. He would take her to meet him. He would know what to do.

Gratefully she smiled at him, trusting as always, as he wiped away her tears.

For his plan to work, he needed Dave's assistance and he heard the gardeners' voices in the orchard as he led her towards the summerhouse and told her wait there and try to be calm while he went in search of the policeman who was at Red House.

She was quiet now, but accepted this without question as the right thing to do. It remained for him to get Dave to play his part.

He took her in his arms, murmured reassurances and, trusting to the end, she hardly felt the knife thrust and died still smiling as he went in search of Dave to deliver the message upon which all his plans now depended.

*   *   *

Faro was leaving Red House considering with satisfaction how he had solved the case of the Brettle Manor burglary, the theft of the jewels and the missing pictures. There remained however the missing girl as well as the tricky business of how to confront Macheath.

Today it seemed he was in luck. The gardener Dave, clearing the first fallen leaves, preparing the ground for the onset of winter, called a greeting.

'You know that lass you were so keen to meet? Bess Tracy.' He grinned knowingly. 'Well, there's a message from her. She wants to see you—urgent like. In the summerhouse.'

At last. Faro felt jubilant, a sense of triumph. This was the moment he had been waiting for, certain that Bess was still alive and held the clues to what had happened at Brettle Manor.

The rustic summerhouse was surrounded by trees, an idyllic setting. Here he had sat with

Poppy on a bright sunny day, wondering if he was falling in love.

He could not see Bess from the distance as he approached, only a moving figure in the gloom. Hurrying forward he ran up the steps and was roughly seized. He tried in vain to twist round to evade the hammer blow and fell to the ground and as the blackness descended his last thought was that he had been tricked and would never know how or even why.

*　　*　　*

Macheath looked at the two bodies with satisfaction. It had been so easy, fortune had smiled on him that day. He hoped it would continue to do so and that he would be safely in America before anyone entered the deserted cottage on the Brettles' estate.

He grinned wolfishly as he placed the bloodied knife in Faro's hand. Running across the grounds towards the gardeners, he shouted, 'Help, help. Murder.'

Dave turned round. 'What's up?'

'In the summerhouse—Bess—she's been murdered . . .'

Dave was bewildered, confused and shocked. Assignations were one thing, murder quite another. He yelled to the other gardeners, who downed tools as they headed after the man they knew as Paul. As they ran he gasped out the story he had prepared, 'I was passing by, heard her scream. Man had hold of her, tearing at her clothes. I was too late, he took out a knife.' He gestured towards his throat. 'Turned on me, he did. But I knocked him out. He's lying there.' He stopped, yelled, 'You lads, don't let him get away. I'm off for the constable.'

In sight of the summerhouse Dave shouted, 'It'll be that Scotch fellow, the queer cove from the house there, always asking about her. Always thought he was mad—'

* * *

Faro was dragged to his feet, roughly roused. He had hardly time to realise that he had a very sore head when he was struck across the face. Opening his eyes, the gardeners were around him, his arms pinned to his sides. Somebody took another punch at his face.

He stepped sideways, staggered, evading the blow.

An ugly murmur and Dave held up his hand. 'Leave this to the police, lads. They'll see that he hangs for this.' He pointed to the knife lying on the ground. 'Remember all of you, this was in his hand when we found him.'

There were angry yells, threatening gestures. 'If the village doesn't do the job first, then you'll have us to deal with, you bastard!'

Faro's senses were fully returned, and he pointed to the knife. 'Look, all of you. I didn't kill her. She was dead when he hit me.'

'Who's he?' someone yelled.

Faro shook his head and it hurt. 'One of you gardeners,' he said lamely.

There were mocking jeers at that. Hopeless to try to explain that their comrade was most probably, as he now realised too late, also Macheath.

Dave said, 'His name is Paul and he's gone for the police. It's jail for you—then you'll hang. No funny business or you'll regret it.'

There was a moment's indecision as they all wondered what to do next. Then someone shouted, 'Come on, lads, let's take him to the police ourselves.'

His arms seized, Faro did as he was told. Hopelessly outnumbered and trying to think of a way out of the trap he had walked into, he gazed at the pitiful figure of the girl wearing only a torn shift to cover her nakedness.

Bess Tracy, he realised too late, had been the bait in the trap that Macheath, alias Paul, had prepared for him. And preoccupied by the revelations in his logbook he had walked straight into it.

* * *

Constable Muir, comfortably smoking his pipe in his office, had never been summoned to a murder before. A new and daunting experience as his sanctum was invaded by a

259

group of angry young men holding Faro, his arms pinioned, in their midst.

'What's all this about?' Muir demanded.

Faro shouted, 'Bess's body has been found.'

Dave said, 'It's like Paul said. He came to tell you—'

Muir frowned. 'What's happened to her?'

An angry growl from the crowd. 'She's been murdered. In the summerhouse at Red House. By this bastard—'

'Good Lord,' said Muir addressing Faro over their heads, having presumed quite wrongly that it was Faro who had discovered her until he was pushed roughly forward.

'It's him—who killed her. One of our mates, Paul, saw it all and he was too late to save Bess, rape it was—heard her screaming then and knocked this fellow out and came for us on his way to get you.'

Muir looked round, bewildered, not yet able to absorb what he was being told. 'Which of you is Paul?' he demanded

'None of us, Constable. I keep telling you, he came for you,' Dave sounded exasperated as Muir shook his head.

'I haven't seen him. He hasn't been here—when was all this?'

'Just minutes ago.'

Muir sighed. 'That's it then. I've just come in. He must have gone on to Upton. Let's go to this summerhouse. And there's no need to hang on to Mr Faro like that. I'm sure there's been some mistake.'

'Mistake!' they yelled. 'You're the one who is making a mistake, Constable, if you think that.'

As Muir accompanied them back to the murder site, the gardeners kept Faro well away from him, still holding his arms as if he might make a run for it.

In the summerhouse, as Muir surveyed the grisly scene, he was still taken aback to say the least of it to find that the man who the gardener had witnessed murdering Bess was Faro, found according to these witnesses lying unconscious clutching a knife in his hand covered in Bess's blood.

It looked bad. He bent over the body, guessed that she had not been dead very long.

Faro said desperately, 'Muir, this was a trap, I tell you. A set-up. Macheath was behind it.'

Muir looked up at him. 'You know the rules as well as I do. Of course, I don't believe you killed this girl—'

Interrupted by an angry roar from the gardeners, he held up his hand for silence and continued, 'Just the same, Faro, you'll have to come back with me until we can sort it out.'

There was no denying it. Faro knew the procedure that must be followed. There was a witness to a murder and the accused, even if he was a policeman, must be kept in custody until the Metropolitan Police arrived on the scene.

'May I collect some things from the house?' Faro asked.

'Of course,' and to the gardeners, 'All right, lads, I'll take care of this. You can go about your business.' But they were suspicious and not to be dismissed, following them both towards the house.

Faro turned as he opened the door. 'I will be as quick as I can.' He hoped this extraordinary gathering, complete with Constable Muir, was not under observation from within, but all seemed quiet.

And as Muir shuffled uncomfortably, he said, 'Don't concern yourself, I won't run away. You have my word—and I'm perfectly sure I can find the solution to this problem and the girl's killer.'

But Muir did not share his optimism. He didn't know Faro all that well and candidly, there was something deuced odd about all those telegraphs being sent back and forward between Faro and the Edinburgh police. He felt a lot of explanations were called for, although Faro seemed a decent enough cove on the surface, you never knew what lusts were brewing up under quite the guise of respectable gentleman or under the police uniform. As for the latter, well, they were human after all, no better no worse than the next man and equally at risk to temptations of the flesh.

CHAPTER TWENTY-EIGHT

Faro realised that his best method of dealing with the situation was to stay calm while detained at what represented Her Majesty's Pleasure, in this case a police cell in the local constable's cottage. There, while awaiting the arrival of the Metropolitan Police, he would put his enforced solitude to good effect by writing up the case, perfectly satisfied that he could prove his innocence.

Confident that DS Noble would substantiate his claims regarding Macheath as well as an excellent character reference, he never doubted that he could prove not only that his arrest had been a mistake but that it was also a plot engineered by the same Macheath who had murdered Bess Tracy.

But why? The motive remained obscure, although now he was almost certain that she had been concealed in Boone's much disputed cottage on the edge of Brettle estate. Whether as prisoner or a willing accomplice of Macheath, now that she was dead, he would probably never learn the truth.

Murder had an unfortunate tendency to spread like waves in a pond, linking innocent and guilty alike. In Bess's case, they would most surely engulf the robbery at Brettle Manor to the exasperation and despair of the

Brettles, who because of the murder of their maid would now most likely find themselves being thoroughly investigated by the Metropolitan Police. And despite their desperate attempts to have the robbery kept within the confines of the local police, those shaming secrets and scandals would become sensational public news.

Morris and Rossetti looked in to visit Faro briefly, embarrassed by the circumstances and strangely inarticulate, murmuring reassurances that they did not believe a word of such a dreadful accusation and that they would readily support his excellent character at the trial, if summoned to do so.

Considering that they knew little of him on a very short acquaintance, merely that he was a friend of Erland's, Faro was grateful indeed. There was a great deal of clearing of throats and eyes straying uneasily towards the bars on the window as they attempted a normal conversation about his health, some futile observations concerning the mild weather but they left tactfully without any mention of the reasons that accounted for their late guest's arrest for murder.

Faro was well taken care of in his unusual prison cell. Constable Muir brought regular meals prepared by Mrs Muir no doubt regarded by her merely as an extra mouth to feed.

As he spent his time writing down his

theories, the Brettles' shattered future concerned him considerably less than his compassion for Bess's grieving mother, an innocent victim of this terrible news.

The visit of Morris and Rossetti was shortly followed by a surprise appearance from Lena bearing fruit from the orchards and cake from the Red House kitchen.

Ushering her in, Muir made a bad joke about hoping that a file was not hidden in that basket and then went off briskly to brew up a cup of tea.

Faro bowed his visitor to the one chair and took a seat on the bed. The constable had made the cell as comfortable as possible. But for the presence of a barred high window, it could have passed as the parlour of a small cottage with the necessary toilet facilities discreetly out of sight.

Lena smiled, gesturing away his stilted thanks for the visit and the gifts. Unlike his previous visitors, she came straight to the point.

'I am sure you are not guilty of killing that girl.' She paused and said slowly, as if repeating a lesson, 'For murder there has to be a motive and what motive could you have had? You who had, according to all accounts, never met her before and knew only of her reputation. Attempted rape, is the whisper.'

She shrugged. 'And that doesn't seem to fit your character at all,' she added, and cupping her chin in her hand, a gesture that took him back to her Edinburgh trial three years ago, she studied him intently. 'Such a pity they do not have a Not Proven verdict in England. As you know, it has been found very useful in Scotland.'

The look on Faro's face surprised her, for she laughed. 'Come now, Mr Faro—or is it Constable Faro?' Before he could answer, she wagged a finger at him and said, 'I knew you were a policeman, despite dear Erland's attempts not to give the game away with some vague descriptions of your business here.'

She paused to give him a triumphant smile. 'You see, I have a very good memory and as soon as Erland mentioned Edinburgh, I remembered that you were the kind young constable who escorted me across to Slateford to meet my brother—and safety. After the trial.'

Her expression darkened, the incident vividly remembered. Then again she smiled. 'I rather liked the look of you,' she said, eyeing him candidly. 'Being a policeman seemed quite wasted on your good looks. I felt you were meant for better things.'

A pause with some embarrassment on Faro's side before he said, 'Is that the reason for—for your deception at the masque?'

She clapped her hands and laughed. 'Why, of course! Men are such an entertainment—I wondered how a handsome young policeman

266

would react to a little lovemaking from a woman whose trial had been a matter of nationwide interest.'

Faro, shocked, stood up sharply. 'Your behaviour was outrageous.'

She stared at him, frowned. 'I don't know—'

'Not at the trial, I mean, at the masque. A betrayal of Erland as well as Poppy, your so-called best friend.'

She stood up to leave. She shrugged. 'Betrayal—Of course, you are right, I am sure. But I think we both enjoyed it, did we not?'

And Faro could think of no answer that would not be an outright lie. They were just inches apart; he could feel her warm breath, smell her perfume.

'Why did you come?'

'To bring you sustenance, of course, a goodwill visit.' A sly smile as she added, 'No cocoa, of course.'

At his stony expression, she moved away. Suddenly serious, she turned and came back, standing again close to him. He felt his heart racing and wondered if she could hear it.

'There was another reason.' She gazed up into his face. 'I was curious. I wanted to ask you a question. The answer to which you have now many hours of solitude to reflect upon.'

'And that is?'

'How does it feel, Constable Faro, to be accused of a murder, to be innocent and yet quite unable to prove it?' Her voice rose, almost in a crow of triumph as her finger pointed at him. 'And in your case to have no expectations of a sympathetic jury of men who will save you from the gallows.'

Faro bowed, his expression a calm he was far from feeling at that moment. 'I trust that I will survive long enough to provide you with an answer—indeed, to compare notes,' he added with a note of sarcasm.

Gathering her basket, she laughed and walked lightly to the door.

'Tell the constable to keep his tea—'

'A moment,' Faro said. 'Tell me one thing before we part—are Morris and Rossetti aware of Lena Hamilton's real identity? That she is also known as Madeleine Smith?'

Her eyes widened. 'Of course! They have always known. It was something of a thrill for them, a delicious prospect to have a woman who might well be a notorious poisoner under their roof, an added secret excitement to their daily bread.'

'Did Erland also know?' he demanded sharply.

She shook her head. About to leave, at the door she turned and said sadly. 'Jeremy Faro—have you never believed in redemption?'

A moment later the door closed and she was gone.

He would never know the truth. Perhaps he had been wrong about Madeleine Smith and her role as Lena after all. But somehow it seemed less of a major problem now that his own future was in doubt.

* * *

He had been less than two days in the police cell when Muir told him he had received a telegraph from Inspector Holt of the Metropolitan Police, who was arriving that evening to escort him to London to be tried for the murder of Bess Tracy. Muir was to take him to the railway station at Upton to hand him over to the inspector.

There was a second telegraph, but he was not yet at liberty to disclose contents or sender.

* * *

Faro had no chance to say goodbye to Red House, or to thank Morris and Rossetti for their kindness to him. But he had one more visitor just an hour before he was to leave with Muir.

It was Poppy. A very tearful Poppy, who put her arms around him and sobbed on his shoulder.

He tried to comfort her but all she could gasp out was, 'This is so terrible. I never believed any of it. No one looking at you could ever believe that you were a murderer.'

Stroking her hair, he thought but did not say

that very few murderers ever looked the part. In general they looked like ordinary citizens and, in Macheath's case, their very ordinariness was the best of all possible disguises.

'Come now, dry your tears,' he whispered. 'It isn't the end of the world.'

Her look suggested painfully that this was indeed the end of her world and all her future hopes as she gasped, 'I had no idea that you were a policeman, until Lena told me. It's outrageous, the very thought of it. Don't they understand that policemen like you are here to protect us, they don't go round murdering people.'

Again he thought and did not say that sometimes they do just that, as she went on, 'You were so gentle and kind and you didn't even know that girl.' She shuddered. 'To hint at such wickedness, they must be out of their minds to even think of such awful things about you, a well-educated gentleman, that you are.'

And this time it was his brave strong Lizzie back in Edinburgh who came into his thoughts. A well-educated rich gentleman had raped her when she was fifteen years old, a maid in a big house. Her son Vince was the result, Vince who hated him.

He sighed. Poppy had a lot to learn about the world and as he put an arm about her, he realised he had learnt a lot as well. A few days ago, his main concern had been Erland's

270

wedding to Lena. He had also been attracted to this lovely girl, had even entertained thoughts that he might be falling in love with her.

Now Erland wad dead and buried, the world had moved on and his world had taken a dramatic turn for the worse.

'I love you, Jeremy, and I always will—I'll wait for you, whatever happens,' she added loyally.

Faro was touched but he realised there was no place for Poppy in his future and perhaps there never had been except for the brief hour of a romantic picnic.

But how to tell her? How did you tell a girl who has just declared her undying affection that it could never be returned? What to say, only that if he were a free man declared innocent of Bess's murder, then he had also closed the door on any return to Red House with all its memories of Erland Flett? Nor did he feel that like Madeleine Smith he would be welcomed because of his fleeting notoriety or his potential as a model; he thought with wry amusement at the memory of that brief experience.

His future lay in Edinburgh, and he yearned wistfully for his return to an undemanding relationship with Lizzie, the kind of woman needed by a policeman faced with day-to-day frustrations and dangers, a faithful wife waiting by the fireside with good food on the table and loving arms to hold him through the night.

Painfully he began to tell her of Lizzie's existence, his explanation and her distress cut short by the sound of voices outside his door. At that moment, a blessing indeed.

A final tearful kiss and she left him hating himself for having hurt this gentle girl whom he guessed would have soon become disillusioned by the poverty and daily hardships of an Edinburgh policeman's wife.

*   *   *

Muir was accompanied by two gentlemen and, as Faro appeared to be in the best of health, the constable was taken aback to learn that Dr Grant, who prided himself on his expertise in disorders of the brain, wished to put on record, for future reference and doubtless for Faro's forthcoming trial, the patient's mental state at the time of the murder.

Dr Innes, the local doctor, had been eager to assist him in this consultation and Muir was closely questioned by the doctors before they presented themselves to his prisoner, assuring them that Faro had shown no signs of madness or of any extraordinary or erratic behaviour while in his custody. He had in fact been a model prisoner and had made no attempt to escape.

Muir thought any confession of guilt was

272

unlikely and, bewildered by the doctor's theories, considered privately that it was perhaps Dr Grant himself who was a little mad, although doubtless the questions he asked regarding Faro's background and scribbled down industriously seemed to bear little relation to proving that he had murdered Bess Tracy.

'He is not an emotional sort,' Muir said. 'Very well balanced and I might add that he is quite certain that he can prove his innocence, that he has been the victim of a set-up by this criminal chap he was sent down here to take back to Scotland.'

'Ah,' said Innes, exchanging a nod of satisfaction with Grant. 'They all claim to be innocent, easy-going decent chaps on the surface.'

Grant shook his head sadly. 'Let us not forget that beneath these calm exteriors, there are frequently lurking violent erotic tendencies which they try so hard to conceal.'

Muir whistled, recalling the dreadful sight of the half-naked girl in the summerhouse, which he was certain he would never forget. 'Incredible! So you think it might be possible, that he had some sort of a brainstorm?'

'It happens to the best of young men who have not the benefits of a conjugal marriage. To a married man like yourself—'

Grant paused for affirmation and when Muir nodded, he went on, 'Then I can speak freely, for I am sure you understand that regular intercourse is essential to the male's well-being in body and mind.'

Muir had never had it explained to him thus. He coughed and, looking very embarrassed, murmured, 'Well, I never,' then hastily, 'Shall I take you to Constable Faro?'

Following Muir to the prison cell, Innes whispered, 'I suggest you wait in earshot, Constable. If Dr Grant is successful with this interview you may hear something that could be of particular interest. I believe he is hopeful for a confession of the vile deed.'

Muir unlocked the door, whereupon the prisoner Faro stood up and acknowledged the doctors with a polite bow, Dr Grant, the friend of George Wardle and his colleague Dr Innes, who had also attended him during the influenza outbreak. Although they had failed to completely convince him that Erland had in fact died of heart failure, he could go no further with his pleas for a post-mortem without revealing his suspicions ‑regarding Madeleine Smith and the poisoned cocoa.

Surprised by this unexpected visit from the doctors, Faro soon saw through Dr Grant's questions, eager to prove beyond reasonable doubt that he might have committed the deed while of unsound mind and would therefore spend the rest of his life in an asylum for the insane. To Faro such an existence was scarcely less preferable than the end of a rope.

For Grant's benefit, Innes had already detailed Faro's presence in Upton from the very beginning. Now he put heavy emphasis on the fact that Faro had concealed his real identity from his hosts at Red House by not telling them that he was a policeman.

This seemed of considerable significance to his colleague, without revealing why the presence of a policeman might cause some embarrassment regarding the irregular living conditions of the inhabitants of Red House.

Faro's somewhat vague explanations failed to satisfy the doctors that he was not trying to deceive anyone and the doctor's more searching questions were directed toward Bess Tracy, having heard from the gardener Dave of Faro's continual questions regarding a meeting with the girl and his interest in her reputation as a girl of easy virtue.

Dr Grant, of course, was not to know that his supposed questions to Dave had been instigated by Macheath and were part of the trap set for Faro.

The doctor was also interested in his reasons for being in Kent in the first place and his lip curled a mite scornfully when Faro told him he had been obeying the instructions from his superior officer in Edinburgh, and the business of the daily telegraphs sounded very improbable indeed, even to Faro's own ears, as a piece of incredible fabrication.

As for the doctors, they sighed and

exchanged significant glances. Who on earth would behave in such an extraordinary fashion, sending a lone young policeman to track down single-handed a wanted murderer? Detective Sergeant Noble was obviously a close candidate for one of Dr Grant's mental observations.

There was that other abnormal behaviour too, regarding his deceased friend and the post-mortem, hints that Mr Flett had in fact been poisoned.

Hallucinations regarding the food-poisoning outbreak at Red House, no doubt perhaps brought about by an abnormal temperature during his attack of influenza, were nevertheless an admirable subject for investigation regarding diseases of the brain.

Dr Grant left, however, feeling sadly let down that he had not proved any of his theories in the slightest. He was either dealing with an innocent man or a very clever criminal indeed.

As for Muir's prisoner, unlike a condemned man but convinced that he could prove his innocence, Faro slept well and awoke to his final morning in Upton.

CHAPTER TWENTY-NINE

That evening there was a beautiful sunset, a flight of chattering birds heading homewards across a glowing sky, and an appropriate setting for his farewell to Red House. As Faro had little luggage Muir was wondering if a walk to the railway station might be safely considered.

Faro laughed. 'Are you also bearing in mind that I might make a last-minute break for freedom?'

'I have your word,' said Muir sternly.

'No handcuffs?'

Muir shook his head. 'I trust you, Faro, and besides it would create terror in the descending passengers who would form their own conclusions about a uniformed constable escorting a dangerous prisoner.'

They walked briskly, with little exchange of conversation, Muir preoccupied with his own perplexities and Faro mentally going over the material for his defence and the letter to Noble whom he was sure would send immediate assurances of support at his trial.

At the station, they had a short wait on the platform. Steam and vibrations heralded the London train. A few passengers descended and Muir, holding Faro's arm, hurried forward, gazing anxiously in all directions. The party he expected was not visible but a man was looking towards them leaning out from the step of the first class compartment.

He waved. 'That must be the inspector,' said Muir and, as they hurried the length of the train, Faro wondered how they had been so easily recognised by Inspector Holt. On closer acquaintance, the inspector was a rather nondescript fellow of medium height and build, in plain clothes and wearing a tall hat which seemed too large for him. Its brim came well down over his eyebrows and almost seemed to be in danger of meeting the large walrus moustache.

Ignoring Constable Muir's salute he introduced himself, briefly flashed a card and pocketed it again. 'So this is your prisoner—Constable Faro.' A quick glance and again he looked at Muir, demanding sharply, 'No handcuffs?'

Muir looked confused. 'I have Constable Faro's word, sir—'

A grim laugh met this response. 'You have a lot to learn about human nature, Constable, in your patch. Obviously you do not meet many murderers in Upton.'

Muir drew himself up to his full height. 'You have my assurances, sir, that Constable Faro has been a very well-behaved prisoner.'

'That's as may be,' was the doubting reply.

The train's whistle indicated a slow movement.

'Get aboard, Faro.'

Muir shook hands with Faro, looked as if he wanted to say something important, perhaps words of reassurance. Another glance at Holt, who said, 'Leave me your handcuffs, Constable. I am escorting a dangerous criminal and, from bitter experience, not as trusting as you seem to be.'

Muir watched as the train pulled away from the platform. Nearby were the two girls he remembered having visited Faro in his prison cell. The one he had called Poppy was very tearful and was being comforted by her companion. Muir saluted them gravely and, leaving the station a very troubled man, he hurried back to the police office.

*   *   *

Faro and the inspector had the first-class compartment to themselves. The passenger accommodation resembled the interiors of the stagecoaches on which they had been modelled, with railway wheels substituted for horses and one door for access and exit.

Placing his travelling case on the rack, Holt eyed the handcuffs Muir had given him as if unsure of how they worked. Indicating them, Faro said, 'Those will not be necessary, sir. I have no intention of trying to escape. It would do my case no good and I have every intention of proving that I am innocent of the girl's murder when we get to London.'

Under the moustache, the lips curled in a sneer as Faro went on, 'By then my senior officer Detective Sergeant Noble of the Edinburgh City Police will be able to add his commendations regarding my good character.'

'I wouldn't rely too much on that,' Holt murmured as, seizing Faro's wrists, he clamped the handcuffs shut and from his greatcoat pocket withdrew a revolver. Gazing down the barrel, he added grimly, 'Cannot be too careful with a dangerous killer, can we? Any move and you will be dead—hardly in a position to prove your innocence then.'

The train gathered steam, moved slowly along the platform and halted. Voices outside indicated the reason was for a late passenger. A foot on the step, a hand on the door as a man's face peered up at them wearing dark eyeglasses, shouting breathlessly, 'Any room in there, sir?'

Holt stood up. 'This is a first-class compartment—reserved! Can't you read, you fool? Go away.'

'My apologies, sir, you must excuse me, I am blind.' The face disappeared and Faro heard the tip-tapping of a stick along the platform as the train began to move again. Holt, swearing at these absurd delays, resumed his seat close to the door.

Beyond the window, the sunset had faded and it was growing dark outside. The countryside, visible through the train's smoke, flashed by and Faro sensed that Holt was increasingly nervous, with the gun turned on him, his attitude tense as if awaiting a signal, a sign.

Faro, observing him closely, noticed something familiar about those clenched hands, ungloved for easier handling of the revolver—as for the pulled-down hat concealing most of the inspector's face and the heavy moustache—

His senses became alert to danger. Too late now, he knew the face of his enemy and with recognition came a sickening realisation. He was trapped, handcuffed in a railway compartment, with the bogus Holt pointing a revolver.

Leaning across Holt said, 'We are about to approach the viaduct over the river and you are to make a bid to escape.'

Faro said, 'I am grateful for your generous gesture but I must decline.'

'On the contrary, you are to attempt to escape—and I shall kill you.'

'And if I don't?'

The revolver was flourished again. A sigh. 'Then I shall have to kill you anyway.'

Faro leant back and said, 'An inspector from the Metropolitan Police—well, well, that's a new and very respectable role—pity about the hat and the moustache.'

Macheath snarled, 'Clever, aren't you? Too

damned clever this time for your own good.'

'Yes, Macheath.' Faro smiled. 'So we meet again after all. Last time it was in your other role, Paul Jacks the gardener—who killed Bess Tracy, knocked me unconscious—from behind of course—and put the murder weapon in my hand—for your arranged witnesses to discover,' he added grimly. 'We had other encounters; fortunately for you Jim Boone had an abundance of facial hair.'

And playing for time, with an indifference he was far from feeling at that moment, he added, 'Disguises are well and good but hands are very hard to change.'

Macheath gave a quick glance at his hands as Faro went on, 'The advantage is all yours, in appearance so undistinguished that no one ever remembers you. Not exactly a face that gets a second glance in a crowd. And that has always been your trump card.'

He paused. 'Add to this a certain acting ability—I would guess that you tread the boards at one time in your career. As I am not to be alive much longer, I imagine you won't be returning to Upton now that you have the Emerald Star.'

'Quite correct, Faro. By the time they find your body, I will have disappeared, on a ship far out to sea heading for a new life in the Americas.'

'Unaccompanied, I take it. What about your accomplice?' It was a wild guess.

'What do you—?' He gave a mocking laugh that contained a note of uncertainty, then Macheath added hastily, 'I have no accomplice. I work alone, always have.'

But he had given the game away. Faro knew that this time it was a lie. 'Come now, you needed one of the gardeners for your plan to work, for me to be found with the girl's body and a knife in my hand. Aren't you worried that he might not stand up to questioning if he is called as a witness at my trial?'

'Your trial, indeed. You'll never get that far.'

Faro shook his head. 'Possibly. But it would have been safer to have disposed of Dave—a contrived accident.'

Macheath gave him an angry look. 'Oh, I thought of that. But there was so little time and dead bodies are tedious to get rid of.'

'Bodies like Jim Boone—and his dog. You needed the house to keep that poor girl with your plan to rob the Brettles and until you could use her to bait the trap for me. Just as a matter of interest, where have you buried them?'

'None of your bloody business, Faro.' To his satisfaction, Faro realised that Macheath was getting rattled.

A moment later he recovered. 'I underestimated you, Faro. Might as well let you into a secret, seeing that it will never go any further. I was helped—this time—in my ultimate goal by a very worthy gentleman—a policeman.'

A sound in the corridor. He stopped, listened. 'No more, this is your destination.' Leaping up, he pulled the communication cord and threw open the compartment door.

A strong wind rushed in at them, the spans of a bridge and the glimmer of dark waters far below.

As the train jerked noisily to a halt, Macheath grabbed Faro's arm. 'This is goodbye, this time finally and for ever.' And pushing him towards the open door, 'Go on, get out.'

The revolver pressed into his side, Faro had no alternative but to obey.

'Go on, jump, damn you.'

Aware that to make it convincing that he had tried to escape, Macheath had to shoot him in the back, Faro pretended to stumble at the door.

As Macheath yelled, 'On your feet—get out,' there were distant sounds from the end of the train, the banging of doors as the guards ran along the bridge searching the compartments.

Faro had to take a gamble, win or lose, in the hope that he was stronger in physique than Macheath and that the revolver wouldn't go off and kill him anyway. As Macheath tried desperately to turn him round and push him out of the open door, in what might prove a last desperate attempt he twisted round and brought his handcuffed wrists down hard in a fierce blow on Macheath's knees.

Macheath staggered, recovered, then, as they struggled together at the open door, Faro heard the shot, felt the agony of the bullet. As he slipped into darkness, he tasted blood and his last sight was of the compartment door opening and the blind man bending over him.

CHAPTER THIRTY

For a long while time ceased. Day became night and turned into day again while Faro fought for his life in a hospital bed in Upton.

Then when all hope was fading, he opened his eyes to the world again to be told that only his excellent constitution had saved him. The doctors had shaken their heads, given up hope for the bullet had narrowly escaped a main artery and his spine.

Suddenly there were familiar faces at his bedside. Muir, awkward behind a bunch of flowers, Poppy, tearful, holding his hand but, most familiar of all, the blind man who he had last seen in the London train.

'How are you? I thought my young friend was a goner.'

Faro blinked once, and again. Without the dark glasses, the man who sat at his bedside—

'McFie,' he whispered.

'The very same,' was the cheerful reply.

'Now, you take it easy—you have still a lot of recovering to do.'

'What about the trial? What about Edinburgh—does Noble know?'

'Don't worry about that, lad. When you're stronger—'

Faro attempted to sit up. 'I'm strong enough to hear the truth. I thought you were on holiday with your sister in Sussex. What are you doing here?'

McFie sat back in his chair and sighed. 'Very well.'

A nurse hovered, frowning. 'Sir, you are not to tire our patient.'

Faro smiled up at her. 'This gentleman's information is very important for my recovery, nurse. I will be out of here much speedier when I hear what he has to say.'

McFie gave the nurse a reassuring smile and, looking doubtful, she drifted off.

'Now tell me all, sir. What were you doing down here? From the beginning, if you please.'

'Never got to my sister. I've been staying with Constable Muir's brother who has a boarding house in the village for railwaymen. A convenient arrangement as I had to keep out of sight while Muir brought me the answers to my telegraphs.'

'I would have welcomed a sight of you,' said Faro glumly remembering how he would have valued McFie's advice regarding Erland and Madeleine Smith.

McFie shook his head. 'I made a brief appearance at your friend's funeral, in my role as a blind man. However, if Macheath was around, as I had good reason to suspect, then he was keeping a close watch on you and if he saw us together . . . Remember, I am still a well-kenned figure among the criminal fraternity in Edinburgh. He would have recognised me and then we might have lost him before I checked on Inspector Holt. And, as I suspected, there was no such man at the Metropolitan Police, by the way. That was his first mistake.'

'Where is he now?'

'In prison, awaiting trial for the murder of Bess Tracy as well as one in Scotland and an impressive list of burglaries.'

'What about Lady Brettle's jewels?'

'Recovered with the Emerald Star in his travelling case, alongside a faked passport and a sailing ticket to New York.' Pausing, he shook his head. 'Bit of a scandal about her ladyship's jewellery—turned out to be fakes.'

'So she told me, when she was very anxious not to bring in the Metropolitan Police to investigate.'

'Too late for that now. All has been revealed and I'm afraid the Brettles will not be living happily ever after in their nice new home and Macheath was expecting a big haul that did not exist. However, the Emerald Star would have made it very much worthwhile.'

'Tell me, how did he find out about that particular jewel?'

McFie laughed. 'That's easy. There's a criminal network in Britain who make it their business—and a very profitable business, I might add—to know about such matters. Precious gems, portable small items are vastly preferred. Big houses employ many servants and there is always someone who can pass on valuable information regarding the layout of safes and so forth. The Brettles also lost two valuable pictures.

'Macheath was blamed. Apparently he found these two items too large to carry and they were discovered hidden under hay in the barn. Doesn't sound like him, but that's the story according to Sir Philip.' He smiled, dryly confirming Faro's theory that Sir Philip had hidden the paintings himself in the hope he might add them to his wife's insurance claim.

'What of his accomplice? Macheath told me he was a policeman—do they know who he was?'

'They do indeed. And so do you.'

Faro looked puzzled and McFie said, 'I was doing an undercover investigation for the Edinburgh police. That is why it was convenient for all to believe that I was visiting my sister in Sussex. As soon as I heard that Noble was sending you on what, as I told you, I completely disapproved of as a waste of time, a wild-goose chase indeed, I had my suspicions.

'Still have friends in high places and they decided that Noble should be investigated. It soon became evident from a bank account that could hardly be justified by his sergeant's pay, that the man was dishonest and it evolved that he was in league with Macheath, helping him with inside information about wealthy homes for years, even during his time in Glasgow and doubtless all ready to leave the country when the truth came out as it would eventually.

'However after it transpired that you were the only one who had ever seen Macheath face to face, in that other fight that almost cost you your life,' he added grimly, 'he realised that you were a tenacious stumbling block that must be got rid of.

'Macheath was here for the Emerald Star and the fortune it would bring them both. A priceless jewel that could be reshaped and sold abroad, the fact that the lady was daft enough to keep it in the house, was irresistible. The rest was easy. He almost walked into the hands of the police at Abbey Wood to make them arrest him, lure you down and then made his escape. All he had to do then was wait until you arrived, on Noble's instructions—and kill you.

'He had a very convenient base for his activities,' McFie continued seriously, 'A recluse's cottage no one went near on the Brettle estate. Kill the old man first and take his place. With his genius for disguise, it was easy. He had plenty of opportunities, no doubt.'

And Faro remembered that rifle shot while he was walking on the heath in the early morning after the masque.

McFie went on, 'But it was an elaborate cat-and-mouse game for him. So he set a trap by killing that innocent lass and making sure that you would be blamed. A little too clever, and a little mad, I should say, but hang he most certainly will.'

'Is Macheath his real name?'

McFie shrugged. 'So he claims. No one knows for sure who he is really. As for you, lad, you will go back to Edinburgh when you are fit again without a stain on your character, with commendations for bravery—and promotion too. And, we all hope, a shining career in the future with the Edinburgh Police Force.'

*   *   *

Later that month Muir escorted them to the train bound for Edinburgh.

With a grin at Faro, he said, 'Glad I'm handing you over to a real inspector. The last time we stood on this platform together, I had my doubts about Holt. I wanted to warn you but this gentleman here had given me strict instructions that all would be well, that he and the police officers would be on that train.

When they weren't in evidence—lurking out of sight at the end of the platform—you can imagine—'

And it was indeed left to Faro's imagination as he and McFie boarded the train with hasty goodbyes and handshakes.

Faro leant out of the window, a final glance.

On the opposite platform, a woman awaiting the London train. Their eyes met. He saluted her, she raised her hand, smiled sadly and as the smoke hid her from view, he remembered her words about redemption.

The enigma of Madeleine Smith remained. He would never know the truth and neither would anyone else.

AUTHOR'S NOTE

And so it was that Jeremy Faro fulfilled that early promise with a long and successful career as a chief inspector and as Queen Victoria's personal detective. He married Lizzie, a happy marriage sadly ended when she died in giving birth to a stillborn son. Their two daughters Rose and Emily went to live with their grandmother in Orkney while Faro took over 9 Sheridan Place, Newington with his old friend McFie's housekeeper, Mrs Brook. His stepson Vince became a doctor, helped solve many of his cases, and was eventually appointed as Junior Physician to the Royal Household.

Faro remained a widower and in his later years the Irish writer Imogen Crowe who he met on one of his cases became his devoted companion.